A WALTZ FOR MISS LINDEL

"Well, Miss Lindel, will you dance with me?"

How could she refuse again? "Yes, my lord. I should be honored."

"Yes, you should be. I don't dance with the daughters of all my tenants, you know."

"You ought to consider it. Some of the farmers have very beautiful daughters."

"They do? You make me regret I don't spend more time at home." She laughed as he presented her into the line for the dance just beginning.

Dancing with Lord Danesby gave strength and substance to all Maris's dreams. As they linked arms to promenade, she breathed in his scent, grounding herself in reality. A tingle swept over her, not unlike the ones she'd feel when brushing her hair on a dry winter's morning. Just as her hair would leap to the brush, so did she feel drawn to his lordship. When she touched him again, she almost feared a spark would leap between them, burning them both. . . .

Books by Cyntha Pratt

THE BLACK MASK

A YULETIDE TREASURE

MISS LINDEL'S LOVE

Published by Kensington Publishing Corporation

MISS LINDEL'S LOVE

Cynthia Pratt

ZEBRA BOOKS
Kensington Publishing Corp.
http://www.kensingtonbooks.com

ZEBRA BOOKS are published by

Kensington Publishing Corp.
850 Third Avenue
New York, NY 10022

All Kensington titles, imprints and distributed lines are available at special quantity discounts for bulk purchases for sales promotion, premiums, fund-raising, educational or institutional use.

Special book excerpts or customized printings can also be created to fit specific needs. For details, write or phone the office of the Kensington Special Sales Manager: Kensington Publishing Corp., 850 Third Avenue, New York, NY 10022. Attn. Special Sales Department. Phone: 1-800-221-2647.

Zebra and the Z logo Reg. U.S. Pat. & TM Off.

First Printing: January 2004
10 9 8 7 6 5 4 3 2 1

Printed in the United States of America

Chapter One

"Mother," Maris said, reaching for the sugar bowl. "Do you need anything from the village?"

"The village, my dear?" Mrs. Lindel brought her attention back from wherever it had wandered. Maris was extremely fond of her mother, but there could be no doubt that her abstracted fits were on the increase. Mrs. Lindel looked over her shoulder at the morning room window. "Isn't it raining?"

"Not so very hard," Maris said, though the drumming on the roof made her a liar.

"Cosby says the horses don't like the rain."

"I wasn't going to bother the stables, Mother. I'll walk. I like to walk in the rain." Besides, Cosby took advantage of his privileges as an old family servant to report on her movements. Today, she wanted no watch kept.

Half an hour later, her mother's list and a swatch of silk thrust into a pocket, Maris stepped out the side door. Casting a glance into the sky, she drew the hood of her cloak over her blond head and put up her umbrella. It was not a long walk into the village of Danesby, two miles or so, but she kept to the wet, springy grass on the verge of the road, making better time there than through the muddy ruts of the road itself. She arrived breathless but in time.

"Maris!" A handkerchief fluttered above the shining gray stones of the low wall that separated the vicarage from the street.

Catching a second wind, she looked carefully both ways and hurried across, taking care to hold her skirt and cloak away from the sticky brown ooze. The soil in this part of the south was half good earth and half clay. As Maris reached the wicket gate in the wall, she shook her head disgustedly. "Too thick for planting and too thin to make good pots."

Glancing up and down the inner wall, she saw no sign of her bosom friend. "Lucy?" she called, sure she'd seen that handkerchief.

"Over here," Lucy called hoarsely from a clump of spindly trees in the corner.

The untidy vicarage, badly in need of painting wherever the gray stone walls were interrupted by windows or doors, was a cheerful-looking building, even in the rain, well suited to the family who lived in it. A dirt-crusted trowel, a battledore without its shuttlecock, a crooked stick with a crosspiece nailed low to give the sword its haft, all left out in the rain spoke silently of the interests of the rest of the family. Lucy would sooner have slept in the rain herself than leave one of her precious books out to be so abused.

The Reverend Dr. Timothy Pike had given his height to all his offspring, including his only daughter, Lucy. As a result, she stooped, trying to make herself smaller. She had also inherited his high-bridged nose, softened by her mother's slanted dark eyes.

Maris crossed the long grass, the wet marking her skirt and cloak. "Why under the trees?"

Lucy ran a loose strand of mist-frosted hair behind her ear. "I don't want Mother to call me in. She is drawing a bath for Ryan. He was filthy."

"Ryan usually is, isn't he?"

Lucy giggled and nodded. "Worse than usual, though. He was digging in the garden—excavating, he calls it. He even had mud in his hair. Alexander and Conner combined were cleaner than Ryan, though not by much."

From the way the Pikes talked, one could be forgiven for thinking Ryan was a small boy of nine or ten. In fact, he was seventeen, taller than his father, and had already begun to make something of a name for himself as an Oxford scholar. The two younger boys showed considerable promise as well, though Alexander preferred boats to dirt and Conner had already memorized huge passages of the Bible.

"Mother was so angry," Lucy went on. "She thought he could have stayed out of the dirt just for today, with the party tonight and all. He says he forgot about it but how could he when it's all we've spoken of for a week?"

"I don't think parties make much of an impression on men's minds," Maris said with a worldlywise air.

She stooped to pat the small, damp dogs at Lucy's feet. Gog shivered all over, nose to tail, with pleasure, while Magog pawed at the air, his pop eyes fixed on her face. With a rueful laugh, she drew from her pocket a grease-paper roll with a few tidbits saved from breakfast.

Lucy made a token protest. "They're too fat already. The boys are always slipping treats to them under the table. Father scolds but they don't listen."

"Considering how often I've seen your father do the same, you can hardly blame the little ones."

Lucy smiled. "I suppose example is better than

precept." When Lucy smiled or laughed, she was transformed. Her skin pinkened, her eyes widened, and light seemed to shine from within. Regrettably, she seldom smiled, having confessed long ago to Maris that she felt her teeth weren't good enough for display.

"Shall we go?" Maris asked rhetorically, already leading the way out of the gate.

With an anxious look over her shoulder at the vicarage, Lucy followed, hunched in her own cloak as if hoping not to be seen. "Maybe we're too late," she suggested, half hopefully, catching up to Maris. Maris held the umbrella higher to shelter her friend. "I heard that if his lordship doesn't leave by noon, he'll not arrive in town until almost midnight."

"Roger said the parish meeting would be over at ten o'clock and that *he* was leaving immediately afterwards."

"I do wish you wouldn't gossip with servants, Maris. Mother says that nothing could be more ungenteel."

"Roger's not a servant. He's a waiter and I've known him my whole life. If being a lady means snubbing one's oldest friends, on the whole, I'd rather not bother."

The dogs trotted wheezily alongside the girls, only to be picked up and tucked under each girl's arm when they came to the muddy street. There'd been heavy snows that winter and with the first warmth of spring, the runnels down the sides of the street had overflowed. Farmers were saying it would be good year for planting, but it was a bad spring for walking.

"I should have worn pattens," Lucy moaned.

"Hold up your skirts. All the girls are showing their ankles this year."

"Oh, no. I'm sure you're wrong."

"I'll bring along my *Ladies' Magazine* tonight and you'll see."

"Father says all fashion is a snare. One need only be clean and clothed to be fashionable in God's eyes."

"Very true," Maris agreed, having occasionally when younger, and not so very much younger, she confessed, kept only the clothed part of that commandment. "But, alas, London thrives on fashion and since I must go to London, so must I."

"Do you think you'll see *him* in town?" Lucy whispered.

"I imagine I shall." She tossed the words off. Though she and Lucy had been bosom beaus since their earliest childhood, having met even before they could toddle, there were some secrets she kept locked in her most secret imaginings.

Not even under torture would she have confessed the wild daydreams that often brought a smile to her lips even as she acknowledged their implausibility. Saving Lord Danesby from a runaway horse, boldly standing by him when all the *ton* turned him away on discovering his nameless crimes, nursing him through every terrible disease in the calendar . . .

She would be eighteen in a month. Surely it was past time for her to grow up and put such childish fancies behind her. A month after her birthday, she would be in town, making her curtsy to the polite world. She and her mother would stay with Mrs. Elvira Paladin, an old friend of Mrs. Lindel's with a daughter of her own to launch. The two families were joining forces for the conquest of suitable suitors. Miss Paladin would be in her second Season, having failed to take during the first. Maris prayed that particular disaster would not overtake her.

Yet, try as she might, she could not reconcile her conflicting wishes. On the one hand, she knew she must find at least a fiancé by the end of the Season. Sophie, sixteen, would expect her chance next year. There wasn't enough money in the Lindels' coffers to send either girl twice.

On the other hand, how could she marry anyone who didn't live up to the image she had enshrined in her heart? She dreaded the thought of marrying without true affection, yet the one she adored was so far removed from her that even her dreams were forced to conform to reality. She relinquished his hand far more often than she achieved it—usually retiring to a nunnery despite having never been nor ever wished to be a Catholic.

The most she could hope for, Maris decided, would be to find a man who truly loved her, enough to overlook her more obvious faults. She would pray that one day she would come to appreciate her husband's qualities and virtues. "I suppose I could always take comfort in good works," she mumbled, thinking it all sounded very dreary.

The dogs, their tiny bodies surprisingly heavy with muscle, wriggled and writhed to be let down as soon as the girls came within smelling distance of the old inn's stables.

"All right, Gog," Maris said. She let Gog down and he took off instantly, his claws scrabbling on the cobblestones. Magog yapped, eager to follow her mate. Through some strange affinity, both dogs adored horses. Whenever the vicarage gate was inadvertently left ajar, the pugs would make a beeline for the stables. The horses seemed to like the company, or at any rate, not to mind it.

Maris was also fond of horses. She had loved to ride with her father in long jaunts over the countryside. But upon his death all the riding horses had been sold. Mrs. Lindel preferred a quiet stroll or a gentle airing in her barouche. "Dashing ladies of high degree may ride neck-or-nothing," she warned, "but a gentleman's daughter must make decorum her watchword."

Maris did try, though she chafed under all the restrictions. She didn't mind their reduced income nearly so much as the forced inaction of her mother's notions of propriety. They had not been Mr. Lindel's. "Don't you be missish, Maris. Airs and graces are all very well but I'd rather see you stand up and hit out."

Maris laughed suddenly as they entered the inn's yard and Lucy looked questioningly at her. "Nothing," she said. "I was just thinking how pleasant it must be to be an orphan."

"Oh, no," Lucy protested. "So lonesome. A girl needs someone to look out for her."

"True. Perhaps I shouldn't like to be one all the time, only once in a while."

Lucy's brow wrinkled. "You mean, have a guardian?"

"Something of the sort," Maris said, to relieve her friend's mind. Dr. Pike was the undisputed master of his house, Mrs. Pike having an even greater belief in his superiority than he himself. Even Ryan had acceded to his father's wishes and had agreed to take holy orders as well as pursue his scientific interests. The storm that had hovered over the vicarage while this issue was hammered out had cast a damper over the entire winter. Several times, Lucy had stayed home to pour oil on the waters rather than attend an assembly. Rather than go without her, Maris had fabricated headaches on each occasion until Mrs. Lindel was quite sure Maris was falling into a decline.

Lucy and Maris had lamented together when, on one of the evenings they had missed, Lord Danesby had made an appearance. They had rejoiced upon learning, from a despised rival, that Lord Danesby had danced with none of the young ladies present, having only looked in on the way back from some political dinner and not having been dressed for dancing. Each had assured the other that he would have been sure to dance with them both, no matter how informal his attire.

Lucy clutched at Maris's arm. "That's his carriage," she whispered.

"Of course. We've seen it a hundred times."

"What if he's in it?"

"He isn't. The driver isn't up yet." Indeed, the shining black carriage had its door open, waiting for its master. The colored crest on the door panel caught the light, the gilding glinting over the three gaunt leopards and wavy lines that represented the channel his ancestor had crossed seven hundred fifty years ago. His horses, too, were black and so glossy with health and good care they looked as though they'd been carved from onyx. They danced with eagerness to be off. The coachman stood near them, draining off a last pint.

Maris might have felt sorry for him, riding all the way to London without shelter from the rain, if she hadn't been perfectly aware that somewhere in his voluminous coat a flask had been stowed to "keep the cold out." If it had not been raining, the flask would have helped to "keep the dust out." Everyone knew that Albert Hughes drank too much.

That was the worst part of living all her life in one place, she'd decided long ago. Not only did everyone know all about her, she knew all about everyone else. Except for one person. He alone remained a mystery.

"Let's go into the inn."

"Oh, no," Lucy said, gripping her arm again. Maris began to wish her friend had been a little more diligent about trimming her fingernails. "We mustn't. We couldn't."

"It's all right. I have a message from my mother to deliver. Unless you want to wait for me here. After all, I might miss seeing him."

"I couldn't stand out here by myself. How odd that would look." Lucy shook her head as though a shiver had passed over her. "It's just, I've never been inside the King's Oak in all my life."

"It's not some low haunt of vice, you know. Mr. Granger is on the parish committee; you've known him for years."

"But I've never been inside his place of business."

"High time, then. Come on." It was easy to be the braver one when Lucy grew more timid and more anxious with every year. Maris wondered if she'd be half so confident in town without Lucy to coax and convince. On the other hand, Lucy might find some courage of her own if she were not there to encourage her so often.

"What about the dogs?"

"They're in the barn. We'll get them when we go."

She led the way, head held high, into the dark, clean-smelling inn. The red tile floor in the entrance gleamed with years of hard polishing to clean away years of dirty boots. Lucy sighed in relief as soon as she stepped inside. "It's not so bad," she whispered.

"What did you expect?" Maris asked with a smile as she put her umbrella by the door.

From somewhere deep in the building the girls heard the rumble of male voices and an uplifting sound of laughter. "The meeting must be breaking up," Maris said. "Maybe we should wait. I don't want to miss . . ."

"Oh, let's hurry. I should hate to run into him in the hallway."

"Mrs. Granger's probably in the kitchen." Maris started down the dark hallway that bisected the ancient building, finding her way by following the smell of freshly baked bread. A stairway ran to the next floor on her left, the banister rails bluntly squared off by swings of a long-rusted ax. Some folks suggested that the name of the inn came not from Charles the Second's hiding in an oak tree but from the illegally harvested trees the inn's first owner had used to build it. Danesby had been near a royal forest once and the inn was at least five hundred years old. And the Grangers had been masters through all of its history.

"Mrs. Granger?" Lucy asked. "That's all right then. I thought you needed something from Mr. Granger."

"A barrel of beer, perhaps? For the three of us? There's very little carousing goes on at Finchley Old Place."

Lucy tittered. "I suppose not."

To reach the kitchen meant going past an open door from which all the masculine noise and a glow of many lights emanated. Maris walked past quickly, not so daring that she glanced inside. Lucy, however, hesitated, made a false start, and then tried to rush past. With disastrous timing, she darted in front of the opening just as a man came out. And not just any man, but Lord Danesby, the fifteenth viscount, himself.

Maris turned back at the surprised sounds of their impact. He had Lucy by the arms, preventing her from toppling over. "I beg your pardon," he said in a low yet powerful voice. "I didn't see you."

"Oh!" Lucy breathed. "Oh, no."

Feeling keenly her friend's embarrassment, Maris hastened back. "Lucy, what happened?"

"It was my fault," Lord Danesby said. "Coming out into this dark hallway, I didn't see Miss Pike."

Kenton Danesby looked up as he spoke and saw the other young lady very clearly. She had just stepped into the light shed from all those candles in the main taproom. Young, taller than average, and remarkably pretty with a warm, full mouth, she was also slightly damp about the shoulders and hem. She wore no hat and her blond hair, made curly perhaps by the rain, escaped in wisps from a too-tight chignon, giving her face a nimbus of gold like a halo. For one foolish instant, his heart caught. "Miss . . . Miss Lindel, isn't it?"

Then, even as he watched, the angel blushed, stammered something inarticulate, took hold of her tottering friend, and hurried away. Damningly, a giggle floated back to him. Lord Danesby shrugged and headed out to his waiting coach.

Chapter Two

Maris hurried back through the wet grass to Finchley Old Place, her hand pressed against her side under her cloak. A bundle of letters sheltered there against the now-and-again rain that still sprinkled the countryside. A rainbow glowed in the mixture of rain and sun, but Maris only frowned at it. She tried hard not to think about the meeting in the passage. Every time she did, she wriggled in shame. She hadn't even spoken to him, not a word! So much for her fine dreams.

Her mother called to her as she started up the stairs to her room. Maris hesitated and turned back. She took up the letters again from the gleaming table in the hall. Some sprays of cherry blossom from the orchard were upright in a tall vase. Her mother was always bringing bits of greenery into the house despite the housekeeper's contention that they made the place untidy. Maris brushed her fingers over the pale pink flowers.

It was said in the village that Lord Danesby kept a splendid greenhouse up at the manor and that he had fresh fruit and flowers even in the deepest parts of winter. How magical and wonderful it must be, she thought, to be able to give your mother a lapful of roses in January, though she herself preferred the wild disarray of flowers growing by hedge or bank.

With this thought in mind, she went into the drawing room. The mulberry-colored curtains were thrown wide and Mrs. Lindel sat in a pool of sunshine. Around her on every side were trunks, carried down from the attics and up from the lumber room. Spilling out of the trunks, like a rainbow on the floor, were great swaths of fabric.

"There you are, dearest," Mrs. Lindel said, putting up her cheek to be saluted. "Did you ask Mrs. Granger about the tonic?"

"Yes, Mother. She'll send a bottle over once it has cooled."

"Oh? Did she make some up fresh?"

"She didn't quite like the color of the last batch. She thought it would lack strength."

"Excellent. Poor Mrs. Cosby's in a very bad way. Her sneezing is fit to carry off the roof and her poor eyes are so red there's not a soul alive who wouldn't believe she'd been stealing the port."

"Poor Mrs. Cosby. Every year her rose cold seems to grow worse."

"Mrs. Granger's tonic will set her to rights. What's that? The post?"

"Yes. There's a letter from Uncle Shelley. I hope nothing is wrong in Sheffield."

Mrs. Lindel reached in her pocket for her magnifying lenses. As she slipped the point of her scissors under the flap, she commented on how ruinous this was to them. "I do wish John had been more attentive at school. His hand grows ever more difficult to distinguish."

Maris smiled, trying to picture her mother's brother as a small boy laboring to form perfect

loops with an uncooperative pen. Now he was
broad-shouldered, though not tall, gray-haired, and
proprietor of the most luxurious white mustache in
the North of England. He had no children of his
own, having only recently married for the first time
to a young widow. He'd spent his early life building
up a prosperous business, creating and importing
the copperware which was then silver-plated in the
great workshops of Sheffield.

"What does he write?" Maris asked when she saw
the smile awakening on her mother's face.

"He can send the coach for us, but only as far as
London. So Sophie will be able to make the journey
north in greater comfort as well as saving us the
price of a fare for her and a maid."

"Best of all," Maris added, "Sophie will be able to
spend a few days in London. She'll be in alt when
she finds out. Where is she?"

"Reading, of course. But come," Mrs. Lindel said,
rising to her feet. "We'll tell her the good news
later." Leaving the letter on her chair, she pulled
out from an opened chest an unraveling length of
thin white silk.

"What is all this, Mother?"

"Dress lengths, goose."

"So I can see," Maris said with a smile on the edge
of laughter. "What are they for?"

In one voice, they answered, "Dresses."

Maris's younger sister entered the room as they
laughed. She raised her head from the book held
open a few inches in front of her nose, showing a
face very similar to Maris's own. Her hair was
darker, shading into brown rather than her sister's
honey tones. As though to compensate, her eyes
were a deeper blue, when one could see them. Most

of the time, they were down, unceasingly tracing over lines of print. Furthermore, her cheeks were slightly plumper and lit by a pretty shade of rose.

"There you are, Sophie. Good news."

"Oh?" Her reaction to the treat in store was typical. "Ah, excellent. I shall be able to visit the bookshops."

"You are such a bluestocking," Maris said, giving her sister a squeeze round the shoulders. "What about plays? Milliners? The fascinations of bazaars and pantheons and emporia?"

"Those too," Sophie agreed. "But first, the bookshops. I can't think what Father was about to purchase only the first two volumes of so many three-volume books. And not only novels, though they are perhaps the most frustrating."

"It wasn't your father's fault," their mother said. "When your grandfather died, the books were divided among his heirs."

"What a foolish arrangement," Sophie said bitterly. "They should have all been left to me. I'm the only member of this family who reads."

"You weren't born yet, dearest. Besides, you know perfectly well you never looked at a book until two years ago."

"Well, I like them very much now."

Maris gave her sister another hug. Scarcely more than a year apart in age, they had grown up with a special kind of closeness, second only to twins. When, two years ago, a particularly violent fever had laid hold of Sophie, everyone had despaired of her life. This illness, coming so soon after Mr. Lindel's death, had rocked the foundations of their lives.

When she'd emerged from her illness, she'd been much changed. Wan, weak, easily tired, she could scarcely bear the effort of even a desultory conversation. So Maris had begun to read to her. Her former impatience and quickness of thought translated itself into a fierce eagerness to learn the end of the story before Maris could possibly read the whole thing. As soon as the doctor approved, she'd begun reading everything in the house, despite her mother's fears for her eyesight. Yet in other ways, she remained the same.

Therefore, when her mother began to display the various fabrics stored in the trunks, she put down her book and took full part in the selection. Mrs. Lindel draped and pinned, deciding a dark blue silk was too heavy for Maris, but right for Sophie, or that the cherry blossom pink washed out Sophie but brought out Maris's golden highlights.

"Must all mine be put away until next year, Mother?" Sophie asked plaintively as they folded up the pieces, almost dancing as they came together and parted, shaking out and flattening down the material.

"I think Sophie should have a few new dresses, Mother," Maris added. "She's grown quite another inch and there's next to nothing more on her hems to be let down."

Sophie flashed her sister a look of gratitude. Mrs. Lindel wavered. "Well, I suppose . . ."

"She may very well be invited to attend a dinner at Uncle Shelley's house. I imagine our new aunt entertains guests on a regular basis. I don't want my little sister looking like a poor country cousin amid all those silver-plated nabobs."

"Oh, no, certainly not. We'll make up the blue shot sarcenet for a dinner dress and then the bronze green poplin for a new afternoon dress.

With the Indian shawl I have laid by, it will be vastly pretty."

Maris squinted at Sophie, picturing the gown in her mind's eye. "What happened to that length of gold braid, Mother? I'll give her old cloak a new touch with that." Maris had become a notable seamstress through sheer necessity. Not only did their present finances preclude hiring a dressmaker, but the nearest one to Finchley, unless you counted old Mrs. Williams who did plain sewing, was thirty-five miles away.

Later that evening, the women put on their pattens and stumped along on the two-inch high metal rings into the village. Mrs. Lindel had dithered over taking the carriage or walking, but her daughters' desire for exercise overcame her objections. Maris thought her mother looked quite five years younger with her cheeks flushed and the rigid waves of her hair slightly loosened at the edges of her cap. Several of the other guests commented on her fine looks and as usual, Mrs. Lindel deflected the compliments onto her daughters.

"You are too kind but a woman cannot be thinking of herself when she has two daughters such as mine. Sophie's hair has quite regained its former curl—such a relief to my mind."

Sophie soon left Maris's side to go argue companionably with Ryan Pike. Though he was a scholar, she had read more widely than he, if not as deeply. Though Mrs. Lindel might sigh and shake her head over Sophie's "blue" qualities, Ryan referred to her as the only "girl of sense" he knew. Looking at the serious, too-thin young man as he towered over Sophie, her arms crossed as she shook her head at him, Maris wondered if Ryan had ever noticed that her sister was never more beautiful than when she made a valid point. Probably not. Ryan thought nothing of living beauty, for his heart was given to old bones.

Mrs. Pike bustled up, a nervous and distracted hostess in blue damask. "Ah, there you are, Ellen. I made sure I should hear the carriage."

"We walked, Margaret."

"Walked? Gracious, how intrepid. I vow I have hardly stepped foot outside today, what with the preparations and those children of mine driving me to distraction. Here's Ryan having all but outgrown his evening wear—again! And I don't know what Lucy thinks she's doing. I have asked her half a dozen times to come down——" She turned abruptly to Maris. "She's in her room. Will you ask her to join us please? She must play the pianoforte for Mrs. Robinson's flute."

"Certainly," Maris said with a bobbed curtsy. What could be wrong with Lucy? She'd been perfectly all right when they'd parted this afternoon. She had not forgotten to bring her copy of the *Ladies' Magazine* to show Lucy.

She called out, "Lucy? It's Maris," as she rapped gently at the white-painted door. The sound of more arrivals floated up the stairs behind her. This was the first evening party of the spring and all the Pikes' friends and the more superior of the parishioners had accepted the invitation. The winter had been long and dreary with endemic colds sweeping through the local population with extraordinary vehemence.

Mrs. Lindel had kept Sophie at home more often than not, fearful of a return of fever. The weather had turned so brutal by the New Year that they'd been unable to go to even the local entertainments. Party after party had been canceled and even church had been a struggle. Maris couldn't imagine why Lucy wouldn't be downstairs, greeting all the people she hadn't seen for at least two months.

Lucy opened the door slowly, peering around the edge. When she saw Maris alone, she stood aside to let her in.

She was dressed in her best gown, a sky blue dimity that Maris had only seen once before. It became her well, except for a small lace trimming that made her seem a trifle younger than her years. "Your mother sent me," Maris said. "Everyone is here."

"I know." She cast an anxious glance into the hall as she shut her door. "Maris," she said intently, "do you think anyone saw what happened today?"

"Only me."

Lucy put her forefinger to her lips and worried the nail. "What about the other members of the parish committee? They must have seen something."

"I doubt they took any notice, if they could see well enough to see anything at all. I've heard the punch flows with great freedom at their meetings."

"He didn't seem the worse for drink." There was still only one "he."

Lucy had been too shaken this afternoon to answer any of the questions that had leapt into Maris's mind. Now she ventured one. "What did he look like, close to?"

"I hardly know. Everything happened so quickly."

"You must have taken a good look at him when he held you."

"He didn't!"

"Well, 'caught' you then," Marisa said, choosing

her words with greater care. "You must have seen him then."

"I don't know. I think . . . his eyes were blue. The light was very bad."

Maris could only think that if she'd had Lucy's opportunity she should have memorized every feature. Of course, she knew in a general way what Lord Danesby looked like. She'd been stealing every chance to obtain a glimpse of him for the past two years, ever since she'd decided he possessed all the qualities of her ideal. However, she had never come within ten feet of him. It seemed more than a little unfair that Lucy, who never would have thought of Lord Danesby if not for her, should have been the one to feel his touch and look into his face. If only Lucy had been a trifle bolder! She'd had so many opportunities while engaged about the parish to observe him closely, yet had always shyly kept her eyes down.

In a few moments, after Lucy finished patting her hair into place, the two girls went downstairs. As usual the main entertainment was talking about absent friends and distant relations. Maris had never taken very much interest in the conversations of what she still called "adults." But now, as Lucy drifted off to join the younger set, she found herself listening. As suddenly as a finger snap, what had always been background noise to her own small doings became intelligible. It was as though she'd woken up one morning gifted with an understanding of a language that had always been foreign.

"Of course it's his duty to the land to marry and found his nursery," Dr. Pike said. "A fine thing if the title should end with him after existing so long."

"Yes," Mrs. Harley said, nodding her plume at

Lucy's father. "A proper mistress for the manor would take a lead in village affairs, just as Lord Danesby's mother did. Not that Mrs. Pike doesn't serve us perfectly well . . ."

The vicar made a placating gesture. "Ah, but people are more willing to follow the lead of a titled lady. I have seen even the most acrimonious discussion turn to the lowing of ewe lambs by the sound of an aristocratic voice."

"A family at the manor would be a better thing for the village, sure enough." Mr. Harley, the village grocer and draper, puffed up his waistcoat as he agreed with his wife. "A bachelor doesn't order more than a bottle of embrocation once a blue moon, so to speak. With a lady at the manor and maybe children in time, there'd be some point to carrying a choicer selection of dress material, say, or patent medicines. Yes, and ladies' maids and nurses need somewhere to buy their ribbons and furbelows."

He seemed lost in a dream of an endless succession of women trooping into his shop to buy trinkets. Maris thought it very unfair of him to withhold these luxuries until Lord Danesby married. What about the young women who lived here now?

"It's nothing but laziness," gray-haired Miss Menthrip said with a thump of her black walnut walking stick. "These young men have no consideration for the future. What right does a man of nearly thirty have to be unmarried?"

Maris reflected that if a village, the economy, and the needs of the land were all resting on her marriage, she'd be tempted to run away from home. She could hardly blame Lord Danesby for putting off the evil day as long as possible. Besides, he hadn't met her yet, not in any meaningful way.

"Perhaps he simply hasn't fallen in love yet," she ventured softly, sure that these mature people would close ranks against her intrusion.

Mrs. Harley smiled fondly. "Ah, you young girls with your romantic dreams."

"It's all very well for people like us to marry for affection's sake," Dr. Pike said. "Indeed, I should hope my children marry for no other reason. Yet life on my lord Danesby's tier of society is very different. There, mutual affection is to be expected after marriage, not before."

"I blame the late lord," Miss Menthrip said, the lace square on her head fluttering as she shook her head vigorously. "This matter should have been arranged years ago before the boy grew up. Our ancestors ordered this business with more sense than we do today. Earlier barons were betrothed in their cradles. There was none of this wishy-washy prattle about romantic love."

Miss Menthrip's brother had been a noted amateur historian who had settled in Finchley upon his retirement from the law. He had died only a few years later, hardly remembered by the younger people, but his sister had created a niche for herself among the villagers. They respected her sharp tongue and appreciated her kindly heart.

"You forget the field of courtly love," Dr. Pike said. "When a knight would dare any danger for a smile from his ladylove."

"A fine thing for a man of the cloth to discuss in front of his young parishioners," Miss Menthrip said, grabbing Maris's hand in her dry one. "You know perfectly well those ladies were married and not to their knights-errant." She tugged on Maris's hand. When she leaned down, Miss Menthrip whispered loudly, "Fetch an old woman a glass of lemonade. All this nattering has parched my throat."

"Certainly, ma'am."

When she returned, the Pikes had gone on to their other guests and Mr. Harley was deeply engaged with some other gentlemen in a discussion of pig-breeding, his hobbyhorse and passion. Mrs. Harley only stayed by Miss Menthrip's side until Maris returned. "I see Ramona Ransom over there. I've not seen her since the Christmas service. My, isn't she pale? I hope she's not been ill."

"Go on. Don't mind me." Miss Menthrip shifted over somewhat stiffly on the settee. "Sit down, Maris, and keep me company."

Though Maris would rather rejoin her friends, whom she'd seen eating while she fetched the lemonade, she sat down with a pleased smile. "How are you, dear Miss Menthrip?"

"You don't want to hear about an old woman's aches and pains. When do you and your mother go to London?"

"Not for some weeks yet. There's so much to be done. We were choosing dress lengths this afternoon. Mother has put by some beautiful things."

"I've always said she's a sensible creature at bottom. There's no sense in waiting until the last moment then finding what you want can't be had. Or if it can, the price is such that none but a fool would buy. How many dresses are you to have, child?"

"I don't quite know. Most will be made up by a London modiste but Sophie and I are to have at least three apiece."

"Sophie?"

"She is to go to my uncle in the north but we thought it high time she had a few new gowns."

"You mean you thought so." Miss Menthrip laid one finger alongside her beaky nose, her lace mitten hiding the wrinkled backs of her hands. "You're a good girl, Maris. Don't let London go to your head."

"I won't," Maris promised but Miss Menthrip did not look convinced.

"I've seen it far too often. A sweet-natured girl goes up to town and she comes back much the worse for it. They get giddy on too many parties and too much pleasure. They can't settle down again to the quiet country life. They lead their families a pretty dance and woe betide the poor fool who marries them."

"I'll be careful."

Miss Menthrip patted Maris's hand. "You're a sensible child. I shan't waste sleep over you. If you'd care to scribble a line or two to me from time to time, just to tell me how you are getting on, I shan't mind paying the postman for it. Now you go along and talk to the young ones."

Maris stood up thankfully and dipped a little curtsy, then, moved by some impulse, she bent down and dropped a swift kiss on the old woman's cheek. "I promise I'll be as commonsensical as I possibly can."

"Mercy, child," Miss Menthrip said, startled, patting her cheek. "Run away, run away."

When Maris looked back, Miss Menthrip was smiling, even as she was waving her cane at another victim.

Chapter Three

No one, not the most experienced adult, not the most well-informed friend, had prepared her for the enormity that was London. Napoleon, the hobgoblin under Britannia's bed, the dark shadow in the garden, the terror of every maiden lady, was banished forever and London's relief made for the gayest, giddiest Season since the Romans left.

Every time Maris walked out from their fashionably placed hired residence, her head turned as though on gimbals until Mrs. Lindel had to give her a hint. "Nothing marks a girl out as being from the country more than gawking at all the sights. A true London lady never pays any attention to the things she sees. Pointing and staring is expected of common idlers, not ladies."

After that, Maris tried to see everything out of the corners of her eyes. It was thus, while riding in an open carriage to the milliners, that she saw Lord Danesby striding along Bond Street. He wore the latest mode of gentlemen's attire, complete with curly brimmed hat, yet it was unmistakably he. Though she would have sworn she made no overt sign of startlement, Mrs. Paladin noticed at once.

"What is it, dear Maris?" she asked, turning her feathered head to look behind them.

"I thought I saw someone I—I know."

"Ah. A friend?"

"An acquaintance. No, not even that. We have never actually met."

"You intrigue me. Doesn't she intrigue you, Lilah?"

"I'm sorry, Mother. I wasn't attending." Lilah Paladin was a girl whose beauty depended very much on the angle at which one saw her. From some views, she was remarkably pretty, with a straight nose, good cheekbones, and a rather sweet brow line. From other angles, her nose appeared too large, her jawline too full, and over all entirely too much like her formidable mother. From all views, her thick honey-colored hair was her finest feature.

This was Lilah's second Season. Maris had already had the full tale of last year dinned into her ears by Mrs. Paladin and had begun to be quite curious how Lilah would describe it. Yet amid the whirl of shopping and fittings there'd hardly been a moment to investigate Lilah's character. She already admired her taste. Though she apparently dressed to please her mother, always deferring to her ideas of fashion, Lilah had dropped a hint or two which had much improved Maris's new gowns. Maris felt as if they might yet prove to be great friends.

"Come, come," Mrs. Paladin said. "Don't be bashful or I shall begin to suspect a love affair."

Maris was loath to mention Lord Danesby by name. Mrs. Paladin claimed acquaintance with half a dozen or more notables, yet Maris had noticed that her invitations and letters never seemed to bear any grander names than Mr. Dash, Esquire, or Mrs. Blank of Here-and-There. Yet after a few moments,

Mrs. Paladin's arch banter all but forced Maris to give up his name.

Mrs. Paladin sat back against the cushion of her job carriage, her face blank. Then, like a candle catching flame, she brightened. "Your mother never told me she knew Danesby. Danesby, of all people."

"What's wrong with him?" Maris demanded.

"Wrong? Who said there was anything wrong about him? On the contrary, he could lead the fashionable world if he would but bestir himself to do so. Half the young bucks in town follow his lead as it is. Thank heavens they do so. Once Brummel left, the eccentric began once more to appear in gentlemen's clothing. As if a man need wear fine feathers." As if reminded, she stroked her hand over one of the egret feathers nodding in her bonnet.

Maris hoped that Mrs. Paladin would let the subject drop, yet after a moment's thought, she continued. "Do you think he will call upon you?"

"I don't know why he should."

"He is a gentleman. If he knows you are in town . . ."

"We are only his tenants, ma'am. We hold the lease of Finchley Old Place from him, or rather, from his father. But we are not on calling terms. As I say, I have only been in the same room with him once."

"But so pretty as you are, my dear, once is surely enough?"

"I pray you, ma'am, not to imagine that Lord Danesby would know me from . . . from Eve."

Lilah spoke from her side of the carriage. "We are here, Mother."

Mrs. Lindel and Sophie had not accompanied them to the milliner's shop. The journey to town

had been unexpectedly difficult, thanks to the very
bad roads. It had taken three days instead of two.
Sophie had been much tired even before they'd left
home, so excited had she been over her part in the
trip. The extra night they had spent at a small inn
where the sheets had not been properly aired. Between that and her already weary state, Sophie had
succumbed to a bad head cold almost immediately
after their arrival. While she recovered her health
and spirits before journeying on to Uncle Shelley's,
her mother preferred to stay beside her.

Maris's head was soon spinning with cornettes,
Scotch bonnets, caps, and toques, tall, short, and
those seemingly worn slightly sideways as though
put on by a tipsy lady's maid. She could tell she'd
soon be completely at a loss, liable to wear evening
headdresses with morning gowns and vice versa.

"However did you keep all this straight last year?"
Maris asked during a moment when Mrs. Paladin
was giving orders to the milliner herself.

"My mother is a great help. Her taste is unerring."

"You've inherited it, I'm sure. Still, I live in terror
of making some fatal mistake in dress."

Lilah smiled with real warmth for the first time
since they'd met. "Never fear. I will catch you if you
stumble."

Maris couldn't help wishing Lilah meant it literally.
Both the Paladins moved with a straight-backed, easy
grace that seemed languidly elegant. Maybe it was
their longer limbs. They were taller than the Lindel
women. The assured way they handled their skirts
and shawls filled Maris with an envy that, alas, failed
to inspire emulation. She never seemed able to drift,
float, or glide. Her impatience to be up and doing

every day seemed to communicate itself through her feet.

Taking in the sights, as every young visitor must, she whisked through museums and fine homes. While the Paladins paused in front of the latest admired work, Maris would race through galleries, absorbing impressions at a furious pace. Not even Westminster Abbey could slow her down. But when she entered St. Paul's, something about the grandeur made her laugh aloud for sheer pleasure.

"Hush," Mrs. Paladin said, shocked. Maris, noticing a few heads turning her way, turned from contemplation of the enormous gilded dome to the glossy paving of marble at her feet.

"I beg your pardon, ma'am," she murmured.

"So I should think," Mrs. Paladin retorted. "What could there be in this magnificent edifice to make you laugh?"

"Nothing. Only . . ." She glanced up to find Mrs. Paladin gazing at her, one thin brow raised. There was but little kindness to be found on those aristocratic features at the best of times, but she seemed to take Maris's reaction to Wren's work as a personal affront. "Nothing at all, ma'am," she repeated.

Mrs. Paladin sniffed. "Certainly not. Now do try to stay with us, Maris. You are too impetuous. You kept us waiting quite fifteen minutes at Westminster Abbey."

"I was looking at the Grand Pavement," Maris said, the memory of all that swirling marble mosaic making her smile again.

"Hardly reason enough to keep your hostess waiting."

"Mother," Lilah said. "Isn't that Mrs. Armitage over by the choir stalls?"

"No," Mrs. Paladin said, staring shortsightedly down the huge nave. "Or is it? Yes, I believe it is. Come along, Maris. We shall introduce you."

Mrs. Armitage was gracious yet a line between her brows seemed to say that she was not as happy to see the Paladins as she claimed. She unbent a trifle more when introduced to Maris. "Your first visit to London, Miss Lindel?"

"Yes, ma'am," Maris said, glad to know she need not blush for her appearance. She had chosen to wear one of her new day dresses.

"But you have some acquaintance in town?"

"Very little, except for the Paladins," she answered. "My mother knows a few people, I believe."

"Ah, your mother is with you? I shall look forward to meeting her."

"You are very kind, ma'am." A flash of gold in a sudden beam of sunlight caught her eyes and she looked past the two young men strolling by to see what it might be. Mrs. Armitage followed the direction of her glance and her smile grew a little warmer.

"Not at all. It was not so long ago that I too was a young girl making my first appearance. You are more fortunate than I. There was a passion for dark girls when I first came. Blondes are all the fashion this year, but beauty is always a passport to fortune." Mrs. Armitage seemed to think she was offering Maris a compliment, though Maris herself was not certain where it lay. She thanked her anyway.

The other women began to discuss persons they knew in common—who was in town, who had not yet arrived, and who would not be making their appearance this Season and why. From there, it was an easy step down to scandals, old and new. Maris wanted to be off exploring the architecture. She'd heard one could go onto the roof and gain an unparalleled view of the city. She tried to be patient, perhaps unsuccessfully.

Mrs. Armitage turned to her with an understanding gleam in her eye. "You'll soon discover the faces to go with these names, Miss Lindel."

"Oh, it's all most interesting, ma'am."

"But you are afire to look about you, are you not?"

Maris realized her lack of interest in the conversation must have been more apparent than she'd believed. "It's only that I've never seen anything like it before," she said, to explain her rudeness.

"You are at liberty to be amazed. Such an eager student of . . . art must be encouraged."

Maris wondered at the hesitation in Mrs. Armitage's voice and surely she'd imagined the slight wink that accompanied her words.

"Wander about at your leisure, my dear." Mrs. Paladin made a move as if in protest, but Mrs. Armitage chuckled. "What harm can come to her in St. Paul's?"

After gazing around in wonder at the porphyry and gilt beauty of the cathedral, Maris noted that the building seemed quite busy for a Tuesday. Many of the people wandering about in ones and twos were dressed in the first stare of elegance. Perhaps it was the fashion to visit St. Paul's early in the Season. If that were so, however, surely Mrs. Paladin would have mentioned it. Also, it seemed queer that so few people seemed to notice the blazing glories of the building. She soon noticed how many couples seemed present.

She, on the other hand, was absorbed in the delights of exploration. Emerging much moved and sobered from Admiral Nelson's tomb, she saw that Mrs. Paladin was now engaged in talking to yet another person—a middle-aged gentleman. Lilah stood beside her mother, that distant expression once more upon her face.

Still at liberty, though promising herself she'd soon return to her friends, Maris was drawn to a large carved screen at one end of the nave. Scenes from the life of St. Paul covered the tall rectangles of wood, picked out in dim colors. Maris was trying to remember the details of each episode when she heard a masculine sneeze. "Bless you," she said without thinking.

"Thank you." The voice sounded slightly hoarse, as if with a head cold like Sophie's.

Looking down, she glimpsed the toes of a large pair of brightly gleaming black boots. Now any sex might wear boots of such color. Maris herself had purchased a pair so she might ride. Yet even though she could only see as far as the arch of the foot, there was something obviously, even aggressively, masculine about this footwear. Nor could an ordinary man, shining his own shoes, achieve such a brilliant gloss. Only a fashionable valet could make it so one could see one's face in the leather.

Advice against talking to strange men had been one of the first discussions she'd had with Mrs. Paladin upon arriving in town. "Country ways won't do," she had admonished. "Men will try to take advantage of a young lady on her own. You must be on your dignity, always."

Maris moved down a little to study an image of St. Paul on his way to Damascus. The expression of awed fear on his face when the light broke upon him was very well done. The husky male voice seemed almost to issue forth from the carved and painted image. "Young lady . . ."

Mrs. Paladin had been right, it seemed. A little more hurriedly, Maris stepped farther away from the black boots. She didn't want to give offense yet it hardly seemed fair that she should be annoyed like this just because she wanted to look at a piece of religious art.

"Young lady, why did you laugh?"

"I think I hear my friends . . . I beg your pardon?"

"When you came in, you laughed. Why did you laugh?"

Maris wondered if the voice belonged to a member of the cathedral's clergy. It was deep and warm enough to sway a congregation and coax tribute of knitted socks and embroidered vestments from half the maiden ladies in London. She'd heard that some clergymen followed fashion. Perhaps he'd chosen to wear such boots in order to fit in with the young men he shepherded. Yet, if he was a clergyman, he didn't sound at all offended by her inappropriate response to the grandeur around them.

"I'm sorry," she said. "It's just so beautiful; I couldn't help laughing."

"For joy?"

"Of course. No one could think it funny."

A smile seemed to come into the voice. "I first came here when I was fourteen years old. The Dean himself was my family's guide. When I walked in, I disgraced myself by laughing uproariously."

"For joy?" Maris asked daringly.

"I'd never seen a place that made me so happy. It remains the most extravagant expression of Chris-

tianity I have ever seen. I suppose I fell in love at
first sight."

"That's how I feel. It's not at all like I expected.
It's more solemn than Westminster and yet it makes
me happy."

"Did you laugh at Westminster?"

"No. Did you?" She began to wish to see the man
behind the screen but didn't want to seem bold.

"No. I've always preferred St. Paul's."

"And now you serve here? What a wonderful outcome."

"Serve here?" The boots disappeared and Maris
heard the measured tread of his steps as he came
around the end of the screen.

Dressed in the best of men's fashion, shoulders
broad, waist narrow, Lord Danesby was every inch
the gentleman. Yet his expression lacked the
haughty remoteness, proof of his superiority over
ordinary mortals that was a nobleman's surest
birthright. Instead, his smile seemed tentative, his
eyes asking her a question that she could not understand, let alone answer.

From surprise, Maris's lips formed the syllables of
his name, though she was certain she did not speak
aloud. He seemed at once to remove to a distance,
his hand, half raised as though to touch her,
dropped to his side. "Have we met before?"

Belatedly, Maris dipped a curtsy. "Only in passing,
Lord Danesby. My mother is your tenant."

"Tenant?"

"Mrs. Lindel. She holds the lease of Finchley Old
Place from your father's time."

He nodded but hardly seemed enlightened. He
glanced over her shoulder. "Is she here with you
now?"

"No. She is staying with my sister, who finds herself not entirely well today."

"I'm most sorry to hear it. But you surely are not here alone?"

"Certainly not. My friends are waiting for me."

"So you weren't merely saying that to be rid of an importunate stranger?"

Maris silently shook her head, knowing her cheeks were an unbecomingly hectic shade of pink.

"I had best return you to them." He offered his arm, holding his hat in his left hand. Controlling her quivering excitement, she rested her hand lightly on his forearm. The fabric of his dark blue coat was as smooth as silk and she wondered if it was. Her head came to the top of his ear but she didn't feel too tall or too awkward. Their steps seemed to match.

Sir Christopher Wren could have made his church twice as long and pleased Maris very much, for all too soon they were approaching Mrs. Paladin and Lilah. Lilah tapped her mother's arm to make her turn.

Her reaction made Maris realize the enormity of wandering around alone and returning with a man. "There you are, you bad girl," she said, though with a smile. "We were wondering where you'd gone. Thank you very much, sir, for returning our strayed lamb to us." She extended a languid hand in Lord Danesby's direction.

Maris instantly let go of his arm, having hardly realized she still touched it. Yet he took an instant to smile at her before bowing over Mrs. Paladin's fingertips. "The pleasure is mine, madam. I have rarely met a more charming student of architecture."

"Ah, young girls are always so serious when they

first arrive in town. May I have the pleasure of my dear Miss Lindel's rescuer's name?"

Considering that Mrs. Paladin had seemed to know all about Lord Danesby when they'd glimpsed him on the street, this rang falsely in Maris's ears. But she was willing to accept that a lady should feign incognizance until etiquette permitted her to have knowledge. At least, that's the way her life had been so far. A girl was always presumed to be ignorant of even the most elemental human understanding until some magic hour when illumination would be shed.

"Kenton Danesby, madam."

"How do you do. May I present my daughter, Miss Paladin?"

"Enchanted, Miss Paladin." He bowed. "If you'll forgive me, I am late for an appointment."

The Paladin women bent their knees to him, Maris following a moment later. He turned to her. "Give my warmest regards to your mother, Miss Lindel."

"I shall, my lord."

"There are no complaints from my tenants? The roof doesn't leak, there are no mice in the pantry?"

"No, my lord. We have no complaints, save for the ghost."

His smile lightened his pensive air. "Ghost? Which of my highly questionable ancestors is haunting you?"

"La, Maris," Mrs. Paladin said. "Don't tease Lord Danesby!"

Maris dropped her eyes. As soon as he had turned in her direction, she'd forgotten all about Mrs. Paladin. She'd wanted to bring that smile back to his face for it made her happy to see it. She wished she might always make him smile.

"Good afternoon, ladies," he said with another bow.

He was hardly out of earshot when Mrs. Paladin seized Maris by the elbow. "My dear girl! My dear, dear girl!"

"Ma'am?"

"If you aren't the slyest thing in nature . . ."

"I, ma'am?"

Playfully, Mrs. Paladin tapped her on the shoulder. "I see greater potential in you than I believed, dear Maris."

Maris's puzzlement must have been evident, for Lilah paused while her mother swept on toward the doors. "Lord Danesby is a well-known figure in town. To have amused him is something of a coup that my mother will know how to turn to advantage." She took Maris's arm. "You have begun your Season well."

Maris had hardly begun to think through what had happened. She flattered herself that she'd given little hint of her surprise at meeting Lord Danesby face-to-face. She hoped that she'd not been too amazed to be polite. He had seemed to be enjoying her company but he was so very well-mannered that she doubted he'd have behaved any less the gentleman if she'd been giving him the most lively disgust of her.

Thinking over her behavior, Maris feared that she'd been much too coming in her speech. A man of the town couldn't possibly be interested in her foolish notions about this magnificent building. How kind, how generous, of Lord Danesby to pretend that he, too, had laughed when he'd first come to St. Paul's. He must have been spinning her a tale in order to spare her blushes.

As she followed Mrs. Paladin's progress, she glanced back at the wonders of the cathedral, feeling a bit like Eve being thrust out of Paradise. In an alcove not too far from the door, she saw Lord Danesby in the act of bowing to Mrs. Armitage. Something about the possessive way she took his arm told Maris that they were not strangers to one another.

Mrs. Armitage looked toward the door and must surely have perceived Maris standing there. The sophisticated lady gave a rather coquettish toss of her head, then turned to her escort. Lord Danesby listened to some witticism she whispered in his ear.

He also glanced in Maris's direction.

Maris couldn't help but compare the smile he turned toward Mrs. Armitage—such an accomplished, so worldly a lady—to the one he'd shared with a little Miss Nobody from the country. Maris blushed and hurried away as she realized the joke must be about her.

Chapter Four

"You are too severe on my country tenant," Kenton said to Flora Armitage, even as he smiled at her wit.

"Is that who she is?" she said, her brow clearing of a shade of ire more noticeable upon its vanishing than in its appearance. "Did she complain of your absentee neglect? You must be a difficult landlord if she needs must track you to St. Paul's to dun you for repairs."

"I believe she is to make her first appearance in town." Knowing well his mistress's streak of jealousy, he demonstrated no more interest in his "country tenant." Indeed, he had little to conceal. Newly bloomed buds were no business of his. Young and tender maidens tended to have old and crusty parents and trustees. Besides, he was not the sort to debase innocence. Flirting with such a one as Miss Lindel could lead only to marriage. Even if he held such a drastic step in contemplation, a slip of a girl would not be his first choice, even if she had the sort of laugh one would expect from a happy angel.

"Who are her parents?" Flora asked as they strolled away over the pavement.

"Whose? I'm sorry, Flora. I wasn't attending." Her words came so apt to his thoughts that he wondered for a startled moment if he'd spoken aloud.

"That girl's. Is she of good family?"

"Very good. Her father was a bit of a wild 'un. The sort of man who 'roars in the congregation' as the Bible would have it."

"Indeed?" Flora spoke so blankly that Kenton smiled. He wondered when she'd last delved into the Book of Books and whether she'd ever reached the Commandments, most of which she'd shattered since her youth.

"My father was very fond of old Lindel," Kenton said reminiscently.

"You told me your father was a stickler for propriety."

"An understatement. But even the most perfect pattern of virtue may hold a soft corner for a rogue in their hearts."

"Then she's not of good family. Not if her father was a rogue."

"Yet I am accounted to be of a good family and my morals have not always stood up under the fiercest scrutiny. And I believe my great-uncle was no pattern of rectitude."

"Oh, that's different. You have a title."

Kenton had grown so accustomed to her unthinking snobbery that he was surprised by the revulsion he felt at her self-betrayal. "Lindel, as I remember, rode to hounds like a man reading his horse's mind, could drain a bottle in less time than it takes to tell, and was the only person in the county who spoke loudly enough for my father to hear him the first time."

"Your father was deaf?"

"Hard of hearing. He was an artillery man before my Great-Uncle Silas died and left Father the lot.

Standing beside the guns for hours damaged his hearing."

"Poor man," Flora said, snuggling his arm closer to her remarkably good figure. Some of it was corseting, but by no means all.

"Indeed." Impossible to think of his father as a man in need of pity. He would have scorned Flora's kindly meant sympathy and Flora, too, in terms both complete and loud. His lack of hearing had not changed his essential personality. It had only added frustration to an already fractious nature.

Fortunately for her, if not for Kenton, his mother had never been one to retreat. On the contrary, the more unreasonable his father became, the more readily she'd sported her canvas and sailed into battle. Since the only way to make his father understand had been to shout, for he was too impatient for writing or an ear trumpet, the house had continually rung with their warfare.

When he considered that the hurly-burly of the common rooms at Harrow had seemed like oases of peace and silence after home, it did not surprise him how rarely he returned to Finchley once he'd attained his manhood. Hardly surprising that he'd not recognized Lindel's daughter . . . Kenton didn't imagine he'd ever seen her before. Yet some memory nagged at the back of his mind. A skin-and-bones child, dirty of face and tangled of hair, looking down at him with hauteur from the back of a rawboned, evil-tempered hunter he would have been terrified to ride despite all his experience. From somewhere nearby, he'd heard the robust laughter of Mr. Lindel and had associated the child with him. Had it been the now radiantly fair Miss Lindel? "Strange the change time has wrought," he said under his breath.

"Poetry, Kenton? I'm impressed."

He had, for a moment, forgotten all about the woman still pressed intimately against his side. That, he realized, was the problem. In all the months since they'd parted at the end of last Season, he'd hardly given her a thought. He doubted, furthermore, that she'd been keeping him foremost in her mind. Her husband's fascination with huntin', shootin', and fishin' left her ample time to pursue her own interests. Kenton knew he was only the most favored of her swains and his absence had not made her heart any fonder.

He wished now that they'd not agreed to meet in the cathedral. But it was a well-known site for assignations. Glancing around, Kenton saw several persons he knew well, mostly with the object of their own more or less illicit affections. He frowned, realizing that he'd been maneuvering into silently declaring that his relationship with Flora would continue this year as well.

"Shall we go?" he asked, breaking in upon her prattling about some evening party to come.

Flora blinked, taken aback by this evidence of impatience. Then her smile grew a trifle wicked while her eyes became languid. "Certainly, my lord," she purred. "At your pleasure."

Leaving the cathedral, Kenton took a look back. Yes, she'd miscalculated by asking to meet here. Though their liaison was no secret, he did not like the brazenness of her move in claiming him so publicly. He resented being manipulated. If that made him a hypocrite, so be it.

She was no longer quite so pleased with herself when Kenton escorted her only as far as her door. "What, you'll not come in?"

"Not now, I think."

She laid her hand on his arm. "Why so unwilling, Ken? You know Sir Willard is from home."

"I must refuse your pressing invitation, Flora. Having but newly come to town, I have many calls on my time."

Those brilliant eyes narrowed. "That sounds . . . we can't discuss it on the stoop. Come in, Ken, and we'll talk."

He bowed and conveyed her gloved hand to his lips. "Another time, perhaps."

"Ken . . . ?" Perhaps she heard the ghost of a plea in her tone, for she threw her shoulders back. He admired her for her pride as well as recalling that she never looked more magnificent than when in a rage, but neither fact enticed him over her threshold. "As you will," she said coldly.

Her butler opened the door then and she swept in, not deigning to throw Kenton another word. He bowed his head to her as she went, then met the butler's singularly blank gaze. The servant stood aside to permit Kenton to enter.

"Good afternoon, Atkins," he said, fishing a guinea from his pocket.

"Good afternoon, my lord," he replied, taking the coin as quickly and discreetly as a market fair conjuror.

"And good-bye," Kenton added, a bit giddily.

As he turned to go down the steps, he felt so light that he wouldn't have been surprised to find himself floating above the pavement like one of those big silken balloons. He had not realized until now just how wearying this intrigue had grown. He heard the door close softly behind him and was hard put not to break into a skip. But his reputation for correct behavior came to his aid, though he could not restrain a wider smile than was his wont.

Kenton found a cab at the corner and directed the driver to take him to Number 32, Ludgate Hill, home of the finest jewelers in London. Rundell and Bridge were delighted to accede to his wishes and brought out their best merchandise for one who had shown both good taste and deep pockets. He bought Flora a necklace designed in two shades of sapphire, the deepest twilight blue and the pale gleam of Ceylon. A woman of Flora's rich experience and sophistication would immediately recognize such an extravagant adornment as the farewell present that it was. He ordered it sent at once, before he could secondguess himself.

Returning to his rooms in Pendleton Street, he found half a dozen invitations scattered over a table very near the large booted feet of his best friend in all the world, Dominic Swift. He had his aristocratic nose buried in a book, a pot of ale on a table dragged from its proper place to rest handy by his side.

"Comfortable?" Kenton asked, when his friend neither looked up nor stirred at his entrance.

"Just a moment," Dominic said, turning the page.

Kenton occupied himself by opening the envelopes that waited for him. Two were from friends of Flora; they went in the fire. Two more were from tailors, inveigling him to change from Weston to themselves. One was a charmingly scented note from a not-so-youthful, but surpassingly fair incognita, welcoming him to town and inviting him to a card party. Kenton knew if he sent an acceptance, he'd find no other guests. He weighed this one against the other note welcoming him to town, a po-

lite note from Greeves, his man of affairs, remind-
ing him that he'd promised to go over all the
pending business. All the notes but this followed the
first two into the fireplace. He had no wish to tum-
ble headlong into another soulless liaison so soon
after escaping one.

Dominic placed one long finger between the
pages of the book and looked up, seemingly surprised to find Kenton in his own apartment. "Oh,
hullo."

"Good book?"

"Hmmm. It's one of yours."

"I know."

Dominic stood up, all in sections like a hinged
easel. He shook hands with Kenton and the two
men grinned at each other. "You've grown thinner,"
Kenton said, waving Dom back into his chair.

"Fewer good dinners in town when the *ton*'s
away."

"Why didn't you accept my invitation to Finchley,
you stupid fellow? Mrs. Worthing would have fed
you until you had a bailiff's belly."

"No one knows when the case will be called, Kenton. I didn't dare leave London for fear I might not
return in time."

"You believe it will be soon, then?"

"I live in hope."

Kenton poured out a glass of claret and clinked it
against the side of Dom's pint. "Here's to the future
Duke of Saltaire."

Dom's mobile face twisted into a wry grimace.
"Whoever he may prove to be."

"Come, now. You have the stronger case; Greeves
says so and he should know if anyone does."

"There's nothing to be done about it now, anyway," Dom said with a fatalistic shrug. "The evidence is all in. It's waiting for the decision that takes all the stuffing out of one."

"Well, come to dinner with me and we'll undertake to put the stuffing back in. What say you to Boodle's?"

"You won't find me turning my nose up at a sausage from a farthing 'fry,' let alone dinner at the best club in town. But what's set you to grinning like a winning tout?"

"Does it show?"

"To one who knows you as well as I, yes."

Kenton refilled his glass. "If you must know, you gossipmonger, I've just broken with Flora Armitage."

"What? Your full-blown charmer? How did this come about?"

"I'd had enough," Kenton said, wondering if even Dom would understand his sudden revulsion of feeling. "I suddenly realized that she'd be as fond of a monkey as myself should it have the same title and fortune."

Dom leaned back and once more kicked his feet onto the tabletop. "I could have told you that, as could half a dozen before you."

"You don't mean that you ever . . ."

"Heaven forfend," Dom said, giving his rich chuckle. "Besides, Dominic Swift isn't rich enough to tempt her, whatever she might say to the Duke of Saltaire. But it's not difficult to recognize that avaricious glint once you've seen it in other eyes."

Kenton recalled that one of the reasons for his friend's present financial low water was the demands of his own former mistress. Dom's case was different from his own in that he'd been in love past praying for. "I suppose I was a fool."

"Not if you received good value for your trinkets," Dom said.

Kenton found himself telling his friend about his adventures in the cathedral, even about meeting the country tenant. "Though she knew who I was, she treated me without any particular marks of attention."

"You mean she didn't toadeat you?"

"No. Neither did she assume a familiarity which so many fools substitute for fawning attentions. She behaved as though I were any gentleman of her acquaintance." He recalled soft blue eyes widening as she recognized him and then, shyness passing, the smile that warmed them as she responded with interest to his conversation.

"She knew who you were," Dom mused. Kenton looked at his friend sharply, something odd about his tone drawing his attention out from his reverie.

"Yes. What of it?"

"I wonder if anyone does know who you are, Kenton. I wonder if you know."

"What have you been drinking?" Kenton asked with a laughing look toward the pewter pot. "Champagne by the pint?

"Can you say you've been content these last few years?"

"Content? Who wouldn't be? I do what I please. I am answerable to no one."

"I thought not," Dom said with an odious superiority.

Kenton weighed his glass significantly and Dom held up a hand as though to ward off the missile. "In truth, it's a bad life for men like us. We've been raised on the dogma of duty. Having no duty to do leaves us too much time to brood."

"I don't brood like some dashed poetical hero," Kenton said, revolted by the notion. "I am constantly occupied. In town, I have a large acquaintance and a place of some note in society. At home, I have my tenants and my roses. The shooting lodge is occupation enough in the autumn and I am never at a loss for invitations in the winter, unless I choose to spend it at Finchley Place." He thought of something. "Did I tell you that my West Indian agent has managed to nick the nick at last? I received an express from him two days ago from Plymouth."

Dom shook his head as if trying to rattle his thoughts into place. Noticing that the fair hair flew about his face, Kenton made a mental note to have his own man give Dom a new touch before they went to Boodle's. Not that he would be ashamed of Dom in any circumstances, no more than he would have been ashamed to be seen with the notoriously untidy Dr. Johnson had he lived in an earlier London. The best thing for Dom would be to win the title so long contested between opposing branches of his family. Then he would have both genius and wealth, becoming, in effect, his own sponsor.

"Roses," Dom said, with no great admiration in his tone. "Gardening is no fit occupation for a man who took double firsts in history and logic."

"On the contrary." Kenton tried to keep his temper. There was no profit in growing annoyed with Dom. He would simply burrow into his books until the storm passed. "They are exceedingly difficult plants to grow. Half the insects in England consider roses their favorite meal. Not to mention leaf-rot, black-spot . . ."

"Spare me."

"Then again, trying to propagate new species would try the patience of a Newton. The grafting is difficult enough but starting new plants is enough to break your heart. I had half the forcing house damp off a month ago. A very promising shade of crimson."

"Damp off? Sounds like what you did to poor Mrs. Armitage."

"Worse. She'll make a recovery, very soon indeed if I know my Flora. Indeed, I'm sure I can name my successor." Kenton paused and smiled at his own folly. "I wonder if I pursued her because her name means 'Flower.'"

"Heaven preserve you if you ever meet a Rose."

"I hope I'm not so trite," Kenton answered and wondered what Miss Lindel's Christian name was. That Paladin woman had said it but he'd not been attending, having just caught sight of Flora. He rather thought it began with an N or an M.

"Who looks after these sickly infants while you are coming the gallant in London?"

"My man Bledsoe undoubtedly enjoys my absence more than my presence, since he may rule the roost without my interference. Yet—alas for Bledsoe—I shall probably return to Finchley Place as soon as Chavez arrives. The sooner the new plants are in their pots and tended, the better."

"What treasures are these?"

Kenton looked around. The door was tight shut. He leaned forward. "Miniature roses, no more than a foot high. I'll be the first in England to have them."

"Man, you are mad. Take care you don't wind up

some crabbed old fellow waving your cane at imaginary foes."

Kenton laughed at himself. "I do find myself growing a touch melodramatic in my old age. Yet collectors are a jealous breed. If some of my rivals knew what Chavez has, they'd play highwayman and waylay him on the road."

"I thought it was only your illness but now I see that all you rose fanciers are mad."

"I confess to doubts about some of them. But if I'm mad and melodramatic, what's the cure? Not another Flora. I've had quite enough of such *affaires*."

"No indeed." Dom drained the last of his ale. "What say you to a wife?"

"A wife?"

"It must come to us all, sooner or later. For myself, I am waiting only to know my fate. There's a deal of difference, as I hope you shall never learn, between asking a girl to marry lands and a title and proposing she wed a plain nobody."

"You'd not marry a girl who sees only your lands and your title, Dom, or you'll have a Flora of your own." Kenton looked more closely at his friend. "Who have you in your eye?"

"No one, on my honor. I have not allowed myself even the luxury of hope."

Kenton clapped his friend on the knee. "Here's blue devils! Title or none, you fool, any girl you honor with your regard is bound to return it."

"I'll remind you of those words one day."

"Oh, enough about that. If there's anything I can do to help you to your ladylove, you've only to say the word. Although, if I may make one suggestion . . ." He glanced at his friend's attire.

Self-consciously, Dom touched his cravat. "Is it so bad?"

"Appalling, my dear chap."

Chapter Five

Late that night, Maris entered Sophie's room to find her sister sitting up, a shaded candle burning at her right hand. Her sister looked around as the door opened, putting her finger between the pages of her book to mark her place. "Did you enjoy dinner?" she asked eagerly, pushing her spectacles up.

"I . . . I'm not sure."

"Not sure? The food was not to your liking?"

"Oh, no, it was very well. Strange sauce on the pigeon, though. Some kind of sour fruit."

"It seems to have soured your mood."

Maris smiled absently at her sister's jest. "It wasn't that."

"Then what? When you left you were so thrilled to be going to your first London supper. And now, you are in a strange mood, indeed."

Sophie knew her too well. Maris let her breath out in a sigh and sat down on the edge of the bed. "Would you call me an ignorant girl, Sophie? Well, more ignorant than others of my ilk?"

Sophie patted her hand. "No one would call you 'blue,' dear heart, but neither could they call you uninformed. Why, you followed the accounts of Waterloo far more closely than either Mother or I and with greater comprehension."

Maris shook her head. "Yet, tonight, I felt as though I were as empty-headed a pea-goose as ever took breath."

"I shouldn't have thought . . ." Sophie began and then clamped her lips tight shut. With her hair twisted up into two tight braids, she looked like a mischievous little girl.

"What would you say?" Maris asked, noting these signs of Christian charity at war with baser instincts.

Sophie closed her eyes an instant. "I would be indeed surprised to discover that any friends of Mrs. Paladin were notable for wit or information."

"Have you taken Mrs. Paladin in dislike? She seems a most amiable woman."

"Too amiable. She smiles too much. No one can smile so much and be sincere."

"She is Mama's friend, Sophie, and a woman of greater age than ourselves. We owe her respect."

"I suppose we do," Sophie said grudgingly. "But come, it was not Mrs. Paladin who put you out of humor. Was it?"

"No, or at least, no more than the others."

Sophie tucked the ribbon place marker between the pages and laid her book aside. "You are piquing my curiosity beyond all bearing, Maris. What happened?"

"Nothing. It is only that I could understand no more than half of what was said tonight. The rest . . ." She shook her head. "Do you remember our French lessons? We worked so hard translating bits of Molière. How we flattered ourselves into believing we'd obtained a good working knowledge of the language?"

"Yes, until Monsieur D'Aubrant came to visit the vicar," Sophie said, her eyes lighting at the memory.

"How we laughed when he first spoke French to us! I was so sure he was an impostor because I couldn't understand a word. At least, he complimented you."

"Saying that I wrote French better than I spoke it was hardly praising me to the skies."

"So they were speaking French at dinner tonight? How rude, knowing you aren't fluent."

"No, no, Sophie," Maris said. "The conversation was conducted in English but even though I knew all the words, the meanings escaped me. Why should they all laugh when a bowl of mushrooms was served?"

"Mushrooms?"

"Ordinary mushrooms in Béchamel sauce. And there was a long discussion about some novel or other. Everyone seemed convinced that the author had based his characters on people he knew and, if he had, who were they?"

"Ah, a roman a clef," Sophie said. "Who was the author?"

"Pinkie."

"Pinkie? Oh, you can't have heard right. That's not an author's name."

"It's what they said. Someone said that Pinkie had written a new book, or the second volume or something. Then they started discussing how much he was drawing from life."

"What did you do?"

"What could I do? I ate my dinner in silence."

"Surely your neighbors to either side spoke to you," Sophie said, shocked.

"The one on my left instructed me in the finer points of fox hunting. The one on my right showed a very deep appreciation of his food."

"Oh, dear."

"They were kind," Maris said quickly. "Everyone seemed pleased to meet me and Mrs. Paladin assured me that several invitations would come to me because I showed myself to be presentable."

"So I should think," Sophie said, prepared to take up the cudgels in her defense.

A gentle scratch on the door heralded Mrs. Lindel. "Don't keep Sophie up late," she cautioned. "She's still not entirely herself."

Sophie rolled her eyes without letting her mother see. Maris chuckled. "Very well, Mother Hen. Send all your chicks to bed."

The house Mrs. Lindel and Mrs. Paladin had rented for the Season had been pleasantly furnished in the lower, more public, rooms. The bedchambers, however, were in no wise notable for elegance. The furniture was a mixture of styles, from heavy English oak to spindly Chinoserie, all more or less battered. They'd brought their own linen, but it had taken Maris several days to accustom herself to sleeping in a strange bed.

A few moments later, Mrs. Lindel followed her. "Did you enjoy your evening?"

"Very much so, Mother."

"Mrs. Paladin says you comported yourself beautifully."

"I hope so," Maris said, turning her back so her mother could assist her with the ties she could not reach. "Mother?"

"Yes, love?"

"You have never told me how you and Mrs. Paladin came to be such friends."

"Didn't I? I imagined, I suppose, that you would not be interested."

"Of course, I am. It seems a little strange to me,

that's all. She's such a woman of the world and you have always lived so quietly."

"Not always. You may not believe it, but I had some considerable success when I stood in your shoes. Half a dozen men solicited my father for my hand. All highly eligible, too. Even a lord."

"Which lord?" Maris put her feet into her slippers and tied her wrapper about her waist.

Mrs. Lindel smiled, looking very much like Sophie in a playful mood. "Not a very great lord, to be sure, but a lord, nonetheless. My father liked his suit very well but I had already chosen your father. What a time I had changing Papa's mind about him."

Maris could well imagine her late grandfather balking at the idea of exchanging a title for Mr. Winston Lindel. Had it been his wildness that had drawn her gentle mother? He'd certainly had little time for the conventionalities of life.

"But that is beside the point," Mrs. Lindel said. "Elvira and I were girls together. We met in London and promised that, should we be blessed with daughters, we should make some push to share expenses upon their come-out. I confess I'd all but forgotten about it until she wrote to me last spring. I was only too glad to fall in with her plans. We are saving amazingly by sharing this house with her, not to mention the expenses of the servants and the carriage."

"Lilah made her come-out last year, though."

"Yes, poor thing. She did not take."

"Why not, do you think?"

Mrs. Lindel picked away a crumb from her sleeve. "From what Elvira has let fall, it may be that Lilah was too serious-minded which did not suit the tastes of the gentlemen. I could not forbear to laugh a little that Elvira should have such an earnest daughter. She was the giddiest, airiest creature imaginable with never a thought in her head beyond the pleasures of the hour."

"I find it difficult to imagine," Maris said, thinking of Mrs. Paladin's small eyes and sharp laughter.

"Well, I'm afraid that . . . not that she has said anything in so many words . . ." Mrs. Lindel's voice dropped, and she turned a furtive look toward the closed bedchamber door. "I don't believe Mr. Paladin proved to be an entirely satisfactory husband. He was said to be quite rich at the time, though I only met him at a few routs and balls. He was a fine dancer, as I recall, quite different from your dear father." She sniffed reminiscently. "Alas, so many fortunes have been whistled down the wind through the fortunes of war. And play."

Maris knew her mother must be thinking of the few thousands her late father had managed to lose at the tables over the years. It had not seemed so very much while he was alive yet any like amount would be a godsend to his widow, with two daughters to discharge creditably.

Maris sat down before her mahogany-framed mirror, brought from home, and took the pins from her hair. It fell in kinked waves down her back, flashing quite golden in the candles' glow. "When do you mean to take Sophie to my uncle's house?"

"In two days' time. I hope this huskiness in her chest will have passed off by then. I should like to have her safe at my brother's before she is laid low by yet another bout." Mrs. Lindel took the brush from Maris's hand. "Let me do that."

"Thank you, Mother. The air is said to be extremely good in the North. London is undoubtedly too smoky for Sophie."

"Her doctor pooh-poohed that notion yet I believe there is something in it. She was never so sick at home."

Maris reached up behind her head to pat her mother comfortingly on the wrist. "She'll soon recover all her strength, darling. Dr. Craven said he'd never seen a girl with a stronger constitution. She must have that not to have been laid low far more often."

"I only pray her heart hasn't been affected. I worry for her so."

"Yes, I know." Maris inspected her face closely by the light of the candle on her dressing table and decided she was not throwing out a spot just yet after all. She would have to ask the housekeeper for some witch hazel. "Why not stay a week or so with Uncle Shelley? Have a good rest. You need it as much as Sophie does. More. She sleeps during the afternoon but you do not."

"They have written to me with such an invitation but it's impossible, of course."

"Why so?" She met her mother's gaze in the mirror. "Don't hasten back to town on my account, I beg you, or we shall have both Sophie and you on the invalid list."

"I can't leave you in town alone. Especially not now, with your first steps to be taken into society at the marchioness's ball."

"I won't be alone. Mrs. Paladin will be here. I've taken a great liking to Lilah and her mother will guide my steps."

Mrs. Lindel was visibly torn between her desire to protect and succor her youngest child and her wish to be at hand for her elder daughter's debut, an event toward which she'd worked tirelessly from the day of Maris's birth. Maris wanted to make her mother's decision easier, though she wished with all her heart that both Mrs. Lindel and Sophie did not have to leave so soon. But if Sophie's health required it, Maris would urge an earlier departure.

Standing behind Maris, running her hand aimlessly over the stiff bristles of the brush, Mrs. Lindel seemed to be falling into one of her reveries. She'd been giving her undivided attention to the business of preparing Maris for London, as well as caring for Sophie, and had hardly drifted off in her thoughts since their arrival in town.

"Mother?" Maris asked, looking at her mother gazing at herself in the mirror, but not as if she really saw herself. "Mother?"

"Yes, dearest?" Mrs. Lindel blinked as if coming out of a faint.

"You looked so strange for a moment."

"Did I? So much to think about." She put the tortoiseshell brush down on the dressing table. "Elvira . . . that is, Mrs. Paladin tells me that you met Lord Danesby in the cathedral today."

"Yes, I did," Maris said, meeting her mother's gaze squarely. She hoped no telltale blush had crept in to stain her cheeks. "He was most pleasantly spoken."

"I hope . . . it was difficult to tell from her accounting. You may have noticed a certain dryness in her tone when she speaks. It makes it quite difficult to know when she is joking one and when she is not."

"I have noticed something of the sort," Maris admitted. "It seems to be one of those little tricks of

speech you have so often warned us against." She
did not mean to criticize an older person and her
mentor, but it was true about Mrs. Paladin's acerbic
tone.

"I hope you were not too coming with his lordship. He is said to be a great stickler for propriety.
His father certainly had that reputation and, as you
know, the apple does not fall far from the tree."

"If I follow your example, dear Mother, I shall
find myself happily married to the man of my dearest imaginings before the month is out." Maris
couldn't help hoping this was true. How wonderful,
how miraculous, if this meeting in the cathedral
should lead somehow to marriage.

Maris rose from the stool and kissed her mother
on the cheek. "Please don't worry," she added,
wending her arm about her mother's waist and
leaning her head somewhat awkwardly on her
shoulder. "Lord Danesby found me only slightly
amusing even before I told him I am the daughter
of his tenant."

"Elvira seemed to feel that you had plotted to
meet him there."

Maris stood bolt upright at that. "How could I
have done so?"

"Elvira did say it was very clever of you."

"Very kind of her, I'm sure. But I don't aspire to
that kind of cleverness. I did not know he would be
at the cathedral. Nor did Mrs. Paladin know it. Our
paths crossed by the merest coincidence. He was
gentleman enough to escort me to my friends and
nothing else of moment occurred." She thought it
would not be worthwhile to mention how she had
laughed and how that, apparently, had brought
Lord Danesby to speak with her.

"That's what I thought," Mrs. Lindel said, apparently relieved to find she wasn't raising a cuckoo in her little wren's nest. "And so I told Elvira." She smiled. "In your private ear, I could believe Sophie might maneuver so but not you. No matter how much you might admire a gentleman, you'd never sink to subterfuge. I only ask you to guard your heart. There are many men in this world—even well-born men—who would take advantage of your sweet nature."

"You need not worry about me. I'm too sensible to throw my heart away on someone unsuitable." Maris had no illusions about her blush now. It spread like strawberry jam from her décolletage to her hairline.

Now it was Mrs. Lindel's turn to give her daughter a squeeze about the middle. "Every girl falls in love with someone unsuitable at least once. It's as commonplace as rain."

Maris didn't want to think of herself or her feelings as commonplace. "So someone like . . . say, Lord Danesby would be wrong for me?"

"My dear child. The two of you are from such different levels of society. You could never be happy with the role his bride will have to play."

"I could learn. I am not so very base."

"You are a gentleman's daughter, true. But he is a Danesby. He may look as high as he chooses for a bride."

"Then it is I who am unsuitable. As I know very well."

Her mother's smile held much understanding and the tenderest maternal love. "I think I can go north now with a clear mind. I know you will be a good and sensible girl. Mind what Mrs. Paladin says and stay close beside her and Lilah. They'll show you how to conduct yourself. When I return to town, we shall have all London at your feet and I shall enjoy your triumph."

Maris found it difficult, two days later, to say farewell to her sister and mother without tears springing to her eyes. Suddenly London, to which she'd been growing slowly accustomed, seemed just as huge, forbidding, and empty as it had on her first day. As their loaded carriage drove away, a handkerchief fluttering from the window in final farewell, her tears overwhelmed her efforts to keep them back.

As Maris turned toward the red brick town house, a wind of loneliness seemed to swirl about her. She'd never been alone like this before. With her mother and sister gone, not for the hour or the day, but for a week or more, London seemed so big and lonely that Maris wanted nothing other than to retire to bed, pulling the covers over her head until they should return.

Though Mrs. Paladin and Lilah were kind, they were not family. She could not open her heart and expect to be understood almost without words. She knew she would miss her mother and wished she'd had the opportunity to talk about the strange ways of society in greater depth. But how cruel it would have been to have demanded all her attention when Sophie needed her so badly.

She rested on her bed for an hour, recruiting her strength for tonight's ball. Maris wondered at her own lack of enthusiasm. Her mother should have been there to assist her, rather than a bored lady's maid, hired for the Season. It should have been her mother's eyes, bright with tears, not Mrs. Paladin's narrowed with criticism, watching her come down the stairs.

Even so, she felt a quiver of excitement as their hired carriage crept through the press striving to reach the Marchioness of Bevan's ball. This was to be the great inaugural event to open this social season. All London would be there—at least all those who mattered, as Mrs. Paladin explained with a titter.

"Do you know the marchioness?" Maris asked.

"We met often last year. Lilah became quite good friends with one of her daughters."

Lilah was looking particularly charming in a crepe gown of palest lilac, her hair beautifully dressed in waves, a Psyche knot at her crown. Yet at this comment, the blank expression came once more into her face. "Hardly friends, Mother. Mere acquaintances."

"Nonsense, nonsense. Didn't she invite you to her birthday picnic at Richmond? I'm sure she wouldn't have done that for just anyone. So many single gentlemen . . . including Lord Danesby. He's bound to be here tonight and you in quite your best looks, Maris." Mrs. Paladin patted Maris's cheek with her kid-gloved hand. It was like being touched by a ghost.

"Thank you, ma'am," Maris said, and thought it time to disabuse Mrs. Paladin of one or two notions. "But Lord Danesby is nothing to me."

"Come, come," Mrs. Paladin said archly. "When every time you meet you gaze into each other's eyes without so much as noticing that there is another living soul to be found?"

"Mother," Lilah said, moved to protest. "Don't tease Maris. If she is attracted to his lordship, that's hardly wonderful. Half the girls in the *ton* have thrown their handkerchiefs in his direction."

Though grateful for the defense, Maris wasn't sure she liked the tenor of it. "I have never done so."

"Oh, no?" Mrs. Paladin was still smiling roguishly. "What about St. Paul's then? A man does not arrive to an encounter with his mistress only to walk off with another girl unless she is of a great fascination."

"Mistress?"

"Why, yes. Mrs. Armitage. All the world knows of their intrigue."

"Not I, ma'am."

"Oh, la," Mrs. Paladin said, lifting one shoulder in a shrug. "There's no use in being missish, my dear. You'll hear more scandal than that old news tonight." She looked out the window. "Here we are. My dears! Look at all the flowers on the walkway. A hundred guineas' worth at least! The flower girls won't have to purchase stock tomorrow; all sales will be by the grace of the marchioness!"

Chapter Six

Maris felt as she once had as a girl when her father had held her by the elbows and swung her around so fast that her feet had left the ground. Everything went by in a dazzling blur, faster and faster, green grass and blue sky flowing together, the horizon dipping and rising as she spun. So did the people and things of the ball appear to her, one great twirling blur in which she could distinguish little for long.

Her hostess wore a rich purple gown which suited her nearly Italian coloring. Amethysts as big as half crowns encircled her throat and, interspersed with cameos, clasped both wrists. She shook hands when Maris came up from her curtsy and nodded at Mrs. Paladin over Maris's shoulder. "A pleasure, Miss Lindel. The dancing won't begin for quite half an hour yet. I'm sure so charming a girl will have no difficulty in finding a partner."

Maris hardly had time to murmur her thanks before Mrs. Paladin had her by the elbow and another guest was being greeted by her hostess.

Their cloaks were left in a small room that seemed good enough for a party itself, judging by the flowers everywhere and the beauty of the maids. Lilah saw her gazing around and helped her doff her mantle. "Wait until you see the ballroom," she said in a whisper. "The Marquess of Bevan is one of the wealthiest men in England and it is said he can deny his wife no whim."

"She is certainly very beautiful."

"With whims a-plenty, if all they say is true."

Maris laughed a little. "If I had the fortune, I might learn to have the whims."

"As would I. But come, my mother is waiting."

The noise and heat of the ballroom stunned Maris for a moment. She'd never seen so many people together in one place at one time. There seemed to be thousands, all laughing, chattering, drinking champagne, nibbling dainties, exclaiming in greeting, and growing louder by the moment. Across the glossy wooden floor, every brilliant color was represented from dark blue to scarlet and that was only the men. The women were more splendid than the glittering tiles in some great kaleidoscope. When the music began, they formed into patterns, crisp and constantly changing.

Mrs. Paladin brought two shy young men over to her charges. Before Maris could ask him to repeat his name, missed among the noise and music, she was dancing, having much to do to mind her steps.

Though she tried to keep her head up and smile as she'd been taught, Maris would have been hard-pressed to recognize again any of the men whose hands she touched in passing. But it was so exhilarating that she laughed merrily as she spun around, hands linked with her partner.

As she passed to another pair of hands, he missed his timing and she looked up into Lord Danesby's face. "Sir," she said with a smile. But, driven by the tune, there was no time for more.

After the next dance, her young partner returned her, breathless and laughing, to Mrs. Paladin, who had another cavalier waiting. This one was older, the next blonder, the next taller, the next . . .

"I must beg to be excused for a moment, ma'am," Maris said.

"Nonsense. As young as you are you should be able to dance the night through without a rest." Mrs. Paladin seemed to be speaking as much, or more, to the next gentleman than to Maris. "Sir Rigby was just telling me how much he admires your complexion."

"If the young lady is tired, I shall be happy to fetch her some refreshment," said the young man, rather bulky through the middle though his coat was well designed. Between the tips of his highly starched collar points, his round face wore a high-spirited smile. His reddish hair bore a line of perspiration along the hairline and he seemed to be breathing hard. She rather thought that he would rather slip off for a quiet glass of something cool than hurtle through the rigors of another reel.

"You're very kind, sir. I would bless you for a glass of lemonade." He smiled in thanks as he bowed, turning to do her bidding.

Mrs. Paladin looked like Hera in a temper, magnificent and frightening. Her tones were soft but biting. "Are you mad? Sir Rigby has a thousand a year, and very likely more. Plus, he is the only son, since his brother died in the Peninsula, and his mother cannot wait for grandchildren. You'll never marry if you whistle such prospects down the wind."

"Need I ask to see a man's accounts before I decide to dance with him?" Maris's color brightened.

"Besides, my underlace is torn. I shall return in a few moments."

"Oh, my dear girl, I had no notion. I shouldn't have spoken so harshly. Shall I come with you?"

"No. I'm sure the maids where we left our cloaks can help me. You stay here and accept Sir Rigby's refreshments."

As she stood patiently holding up her gown while a maid fixed the lace, Maris felt guilty that she'd spoken so sharply to Mrs. Paladin. After all, it was her duty to guide her through the labyrinth of the social niceties. In the absence of her own mother, she should show Mrs. Paladin the same courtesy, if she couldn't manage the same affection.

She emerged, repaired, and determined to apologize to Mrs. Paladin. Trying out words in her mind, she was not watching where she was going. She stepped on a blue satin train whisking along the floor. The woman it belonged to gasped and stopped, perforce. Her two friends walking beside her also paused.

"Clumsy child," Mrs. Armitage said. Then she checked and peered at Maris. "Miss . . . Miss Lindel, is it not?

"Yes, ma'am," Maris said, dipping a hasty curtsy.

Mrs. Armitage's color was higher than it had been at the cathedral. Her gown was excessively low-cut to make a better display of the stunningly beautiful necklace reposing upon her white bosom. Impossible not to mention it, after her apology. Mrs. Armitage brushed her fingers across it, setting the articulated clusters to swaying. "I'm sure there are many such trifles in your future."

"I've no such ambition."

"You seek a simple golden band, no doubt." Her

friends, both well-dressed and bejeweled, tittered behind their hands.

Mrs. Armitage's hostility had no basis, so far as Maris knew. Surely, she'd apologized enough for tripping over her train. She frowned. "Every woman must hope to marry. If you'll pardon me, ma'am, I should find my party."

As she walked away, with the obscure feeling that she should run, she heard one of the other two ask Mrs. Armitage, "Who was that?"

"That," Mrs. Armitage said, icily clear, "is the minx who was making sheep's eyes at Lord Danesby."

Maris couldn't believe that anyone would be so thoughtlessly cruel to someone who had done them no harm. She returned to the ballroom, blind now to elegancies and follies alike.

"Miss Lindel," Lord Danesby said, taking her arm. "You are unwell."

"No, no, sir," Maris said, looking back, worried that those dreadful women would see Lord Danesby with her. She wanted to protect him from their distorted view.

"It's far too stuffy in here." He looked about him. "Come nearer the window and catch a breath of air.

"I am quite well, my lord," she answered, resisting the gentle guidance of his hand. "It's all very wonderful, isn't it?"

"Your first grown-up ball?"

She had not thought that blue eyes could be so warm. Though she nodded at first, so mesmerized she'd hardly heard what he said, she instantly corrected this misapprehension. She was no child, allowed out of the nursery to peep at the party from over the banister. "I attended some winter assemblies last year in Guiverston."

"Indeed," he said, as though this were fascinating information.

Maris smiled up at him, forgetting for a moment that they might be observed and her expression misinterpreted again. "But even Guiverston is nothing like London."

"The comparison is not generally made. Do you miss Finchley?"

"I miss the people. They are dearer to me than I knew, when I saw them every day. Do you miss it?"

"I am something of a weathercock, Miss Lindel. When in London, I wonder why I ever left home. When I am at Finchley Place, I wonder what possessed me to think I could ever bear the retired life."

"At least you are not tied to either one by some occupation."

"There is that. I would be very unhappy as a laborer, unable to leave my position for fear of poverty and yet yearning to be elsewhere."

"You could have run away to sea." Maris enjoyed countering his flight of fancy with one of her own. "Sailors are never still even at rest."

"True. But they cannot escape their ship in the middle of the ocean. I think, you know, if I'd needed to choose a profession I would have liked to have been a shoemaker."

"A shoemaker?" Maris repeated, looking at his well-cared-for hands. "They stay at their lasts."

"But perhaps I could take comfort in thinking of all the places my shoes might go."

"And never go yourself?" She shook her head. "I

have lived vicariously now for some twelve years. It does not satisfy."

Maris did not mean to be mysterious. Seeing his interested gaze, she hurried to explain herself. "As a girl, I mean."

"'As a girl,' you live vicariously?" He tapped his cheek thoughtfully with his forefinger. His eyes looked even bluer when focused intently on her and they were already the most fascinating sea blue she'd ever seen. "As a man, I confess I cannot understand what you mean."

Maris caught the corner of her underlip in her teeth and looked past him at a large sparkling chandelier, seeking words. "I mean . . . girls live so quietly, learning our letters, sewing our samplers, playing with dolls and other girls . . . unless you have brothers." She was getting confused.

Maris stopped and began again. "We have only our dreams, yet even while we are dreaming, we know there's no chance. . . . A man might dream of being a sailor or a soldier or . . . or prime minister. He can sail away or march off to fight or take his seat. Or even choose to make shoes. Unless a girl limits her dreams to the possible, she must know they will never come true."

"And what use are dreams only of the possible?" Lord Danesby murmured.

She smiled at him again, just as she would have at any friend. "Exactly. My lord."

"Don't start 'my lording' me now, Miss Lindel," he said with a chuckle. Then, more seriously, he added, "Would you have a woman be prime minister?"

"I would, if she were capable. I have known women who could give the Duke of Wellington

lessons in strategy and men who cannot give an
order to the cook."

"Lord, so have I," he said, as if surprised. "Are you
a strategist, Miss Lindel?"

She shook her head. "I am not clever, sir. I wish I
were."

"Can you dance? You must, if you attended the
winter assemblies at Guiverston. Will you honor me,
Miss Lindel?"

Maris recalled with a sense of shock that they
were not alone. Quite the reverse. She stole a look
about her. As she feared, this long chat had not
gone unwitnessed. All about them, women whispered behind their fans while a few were even so
vulgar as to stretch upon their tiptoes in order to
see over their taller sisters. As the flush mounted
into her cheeks, she stammered out a plea to return
to her friends.

"You won't dance with me?" Was he offended?
She stole a peek at his face and saw confusion but
no lack of amusement. "I assure you that your com-
panions won't object to me."

Thinking of Mrs. Paladin's rapture at his notice
of her, Maris did not doubt that Lord Danesby
would prove acceptable in every way. If she were
here now, no question but that she would be urging
Maris to accept at once. Even more intently did her
heart wish it. To dance with him, just once, would
be as near to a dream as any waking experience
could be.

"It's not Mrs. Paladin's objections that concern
me, sir." She dropped her voice to a whisper. "It's
the notice of the larger world."

Now he looked about them as well. She saw his

chin lift with pride even as his strong brows drew together. "Shall I tell you my family motto?"

"'Flinch not nor fear,'" Maris said, her own chin rising.

"Would you mind telling me just how you know that?" he asked sharply as her words passed over his.

"It's carved into the stone lintel over the front door at Finchley Old Place, as well as over the fireplace in the kitchen. Did you forget my mother is your tenant?"

"Yes, I did. Tell me, is she here tonight?"

"No, she's gone out of town." She explained briefly about Sophie and her uncle's invitation.

"I see. I will call on her when she returns. I have something of particular import to discuss with her." She looked up at him interrogatively but he shook his head. "Well, Miss Lindel, will you dance with me?"

How could she refuse again? "Yes, my lord. I should be honored."

"Yes, you should be. I don't dance with the daughters of all my tenants, you know."

"You ought to consider it. Some of the farmers have very beautiful daughters."

"They do? You make me regret I don't spend more time at home." She laughed as he presented her into the line for the dance just beginning.

Dancing with Lord Danesby gave strength and substance to all Maris's dreams. As they linked arms to promenade, she breathed in his scent, grounding herself in reality. A tingle swept over her, not unlike the ones she'd feel when brushing her hair on a dry winter's morning. Just as her hair would leap to the brush, so did she feel drawn to his lordship. When she touched him again, she almost feared a spark would leap between them, burning them both.

Maris was at least spared the fear of tripping or stepping on his toes. Though not possessed of Lilah Paladin's languid grace, she could dance well and, moreover, she enjoyed the exercise. It wasn't riding, but it was better than most of London life. Lord Danesby, too, seemed to smile rather more at her than with the others he met in the course of the steps, though that may have just been his polite way of honoring his partner.

When it ended, all too soon, he stood with her for a moment, both of them breathing hard. "Shall we attempt the second half of the set?" he asked.

"I'm game for it, if you are."

Just then, two ladies walked by. Maris had been introduced to them earlier in the evening and she gave them a nod and a smile. The smile faded when one looked at her with half-closed eyes and gave a small but audible sniff. The other murmured, "Some girls waste no time."

Puzzled, Maris looked at Lord Danesby. He stared after the ladies, an eyebrow lifted. "What was that about?" he asked.

"I have no notion. Do you know them?"

"Very well indeed. One is a distant cousin on the distaff side, the other her longtime bosom companion." His smile returned. "Never mind. Shall we dance again?"

Maris wanted to accept, very badly. But she felt chilled, not by the temperature of the room itself but by a change of atmosphere. Everywhere she looked, she met censorious gazes. "I had better return to Mrs. Paladin. She'll wonder what became of me."

"I'll take you to her at once. Er . . . where is she?"

He tucked her arm under his own and held her to a pace more moderate than she would have chosen. "Slowly, slowly, Miss Lindel. If the world wishes to stare, let it look its fill."

"Why should they wish to stare at me?"

"You may wrong yourself. It may be myself they wish to observe. This new way of tying my cravat is most unusual. No doubt everyone wishes to study it in detail."

"You sound like a coxcomb, my lord."

"Dandy, my dear child, dandy. Alas, that I forgot my quizzing glass for I'd soon make a few souls look blue." Lord Danesby may have sounded like a lazy-voiced dandy but his eyes were that of a giddy boy.

"They'll never believe me at home when I write them about tonight," Maris said, hardly realizing she had spoken aloud. "It's like a fairy tale."

"I've never been the hero of a fairy tale before," Lord Danesby said, the faintest tinge of bitterness seeping into his tone. "We viscounts are usually found in fiction as wicked uncles trying to chouse the heroine out of her fortune."

"I only meant . . . they think of you as someone so unapproachable and haughty. You don't mingle very much with the townsfolk, after all."

"I hope I do my duty by them."

"Oh, you do. The new pulpit is very much admired. Dr. Pike hurt his shin so badly when the old one gave way. No one had had any notion of how completely it had rotted."

"Fifteenth century, wasn't it?"

"I believe so." Maris felt a little guilty for never listening when Dr. Pike droned on about the history of their little church.

"I did try to find some craftsmen who could make something in keeping with the period of the original but the war made it impossible to import Italian artisans, as my grandfather would have done."

"The modern one is more to my taste," Maris said. "Antiques are so gloomy."

"Yes," Lord Danesby said, his steps slowing even further as he pondered this. "Finchley Place is full of antiques and it's very gloomy indeed. I don't believe my ancestors ever discarded anything, from a full suit of parade armor to my school reports."

"You should have seen all the dress material my mother had hoarded against the day of my debut. Trunks and trunks of it, all dragged out into the middle of the floor and strewn about the room."

"She must regret, very much, not being here tonight."

"I regret it more but my sister's constitution cannot support London at present. I only hope she recovers her strength before she must appear herself."

"Will you attend a Drawing Room this year?"

"I don't know but I certainly hope not," she said, leaning in to speak more softly. Mrs. Paladin had been shocked by her radical notions. "The thought of making my curtsy to the Queen while wearing hoops and feathers terrifies me. I'd be bound to go over like a ninepin!"

His eyes laughed at her image. "Does Almack's also terrify you?"

"Even more so than a Drawing Room. Besides, Mrs. Paladin says it's impossible to acquire vouchers lately. She has been turned down twice and says it's useless to ask again until some weeks have passed."

"Yes, I imagine it must be. I would intercede on

your behalf but that is something no single gentleman could do for a young lady to whom he was not
related."

"That would cause terrible gossip, wouldn't it?"

"Terrible. It would be tantamount to a public proposal."

They were talking of other things, of spring returning to the great public parks of London, of
horses, of art, when a shrill voice called out Maris's
name. Startled out of her dream, Maris stopped
short. They'd walked right past Mrs. Paladin, seated
on one of the dainty gilded chairs against the wall.

Her teeth were much in evidence as she thanked
Lord Danesby for returning her wandering charge
to her. "You are always finding her when she has
strayed away, Lord Danesby."

"You make me sound like a sheep," Maris said,
still in alt from her long conversation with Lord
Danesby.

He choked a little, turning a laugh into a cough.
"So pleasant a lady will be welcome wherever she
strays," he said, quite like a prince from a fairy tale.

Lord Danesby turned away from Mrs. Paladin,
who stammered an unheard reply. He bowed to
Maris. When she arose from her curtsy, he held out
his hand. "A pleasure to see you again, Miss Lindel."

"I also," she said, shaking hands with him.

"Don't forget about my offer."

"You're too kind, my lord."

He bowed again to Mrs. Paladin and walked away.
Maris, hardly knowing what she did, sank into the
vacant seat beside her. She felt as if she'd lived for
an hour on a golden cloud. *He* didn't seem to find
her impertinent or scatterbrained when she said
something out of the common way. If he hadn't un-

derstood her, he asked for her meaning without insulting her. But for the most part, he entered into her feelings with great sensitivity. She didn't flatter herself that he'd found her fascinating but she had amused him, a sweeter service than all her dreams of rescuing him from a dire fate.

She woke to a sharp pinch of Mrs. Paladin's fingers on her arm. "For heaven's sake, Maris, tell me what he said," she hissed. "What offer did he make to you?"

"Offer, ma'am?" Maris returned to the present, the last wisps of her cloud dissipating under the cold light of Mrs. Paladin's eyes.

"Yes, his offer, you foolish chit. A ride in his carriage, an escort to the theater, *carte blanche* . . . what did he offer you?"

"*Carte blanche*, ma'am? What is that? A . . . a white card?"

"Never mind that." Spacing her words out as though to a deaf child, she asked again. "What . . . offer . . . did . . . ?"

"Merely to frank any letters I might wish to send. He's a peer, you know. They're permitted to do that."

Kenton strolled away from Miss Lindel's group, nodding to acquaintances and friends but speaking to no one until he reached the card room. There he found several cronies, no more fond of dancing than he himself, playing whist. Waiting for an open seat at the table, he seated himself in an armchair and took up a glass of wine. He wondered why he'd decided to dance with Miss Lindel. She'd not hinted that she'd wanted to; it had been all his own notion. Strange that. He could not recall when he'd last done more than a duty dance with a hostess or her daughter.

What was it about Miss Lindel? She had a smile of unexpected charm, but many other girls were no less winsome. Her blond beauty was nothing extraordinary; there were many others whose beauty took a man's breath away at first sight. Yet he'd felt that here was someone who saw things in a different light from other people. Perhaps he was wrong, perhaps all debutantes possessed Miss Lindel's mixture of youthful enthusiasm and burgeoning wisdom. He rarely spoke to young ladies, as their mothers were wary of him.

He'd been on the town now for ten years and no woman could say he'd ever offered marriage. The thought of being forced to listen to one woman for the rest of his life had held him back even when attracted. He preferred women like Flora Armitage. She wanted no more of his tenderer emotions than he wanted of hers. Desire was no substitute for love, he supposed, but for lack of anything better it would do.

He became aware that several men he knew were looking at him. He nodded in greeting and they came over to stand or lounge about him. After a little talk about horses, the latest word in gambling hells, and bets on the books, Gregory Haveson chuckled. "Maybe it won't be so long before your name is written in White's betting book, eh, Danesby?"

"My name? Why should it be?" Had someone found out what Chavez was bringing him?

Despite his friend Russell's digging his elbow into

his side, Haveson went on. "Matrimony, don't you know. What is her name, by the way?"

"You'd know better than I," Kenton said slowly. He finished the last drops of his wine. Was this what came of dancing with a girl?

"Oh, come. You can tell me. Besides, isn't she with that Paladin woman? I can't imagine she'd refuse to give me an introduction even if I didn't care for that dry, cold daughter of hers."

Though Haveson was the taller, he stepped back when Kenton rose to his feet. Holding the younger man's eyes, Kenton waited until Haveson's smile faltered and became uncertain. "It seems that courtesy has fallen off a bit in society of late. When I was young, it was not done for a man to bandy a lady's name in a card room or, indeed, anywhere. Break yourself of the habit, Mr. Haveson. I advise you most strongly to break that habit."

Kenton put down both pieces of his wineglass, the stem snapped in two. As he went out, he knew, from the sudden rush of whispering, that the full tale of his youth was being told. He'd met his man twice at Barn Elms, once with pistols, once with swords. He'd never killed, deloping the first time, and toying with his foe the second time. With every touch, his enemy had known that it was only Kenton's mercy that had saved him from death. At the time, he'd thought himself a devil of a fellow. Now, he could only feel profoundly grateful that he'd never been arrested. Still, his reputation should serve to keep popinjays like Haveson quiet.

But no power on earth could silence the tongues of women. He couldn't be certain they were discussing Miss Lindel and himself as they would stop talking as he passed and begin again the moment they felt he was out of earshot. Though he did not blush, his ears burned like Bengal fire signal lights on a man-of-war.

He danced with several other girls, hoping perhaps to conceal his attention to Miss Lindel as just one duty dance among others. As he had begun to suspect, not even the most famously vibrant young lady had quite Miss Lindel's sparkle. This one might be gay, that one serious-minded, this one accomplished, and that one piquantly beautiful, but none had her precise, though hard-to-define, quality. Of course, he thought fairly, it was difficult to plumb the depths of a girl's soul while contra-dancing.

Kenton excused himself to his hostess, who looked knowing but made no references, and went home. He chose not to drive but to walk, finding the rain-glistening streets a cooling antidote to the hot, noisy ballroom, though London could never claim to be quiet. The noise seemed far away tonight, muffled by the hovering clouds. Yet the clopping of hooves seemed to be right behind him even after he'd walked for some time. Kenton stopped and glanced behind him.

A closed carriage, shiny black, drove behind him. When he looked back, the window slid down and a round female arm, clad in a tight-fitting glove appeared. He felt he recognized the bracelet that clasped that wrist. The gloved hand beckoned.

"How may I serve you, Mrs. Armitage," he asked, when he reached the window.

"It's too wet a night to walk. May I drive you somewhere?"

That was for the driver. Flora did like to maintain appearances, though of course her butler and dresser knew everything. "You're very kind, Mrs. Armitage, but I'm not afraid of a little rain."

"I assure you it's no trouble. Give my driver the address, won't you?"

Kenton knew he owed her an explanation of his abrupt severing of their liaison. Even if he himself wasn't entirely sure why he'd suddenly felt so tainted by it. He'd sent a note along with the necklace, now glimmering at him through the darkness, yet she had sought out this meeting. One thing he knew as he entered her carriage; he'd not weaken and renew this affair.

"She's a lovely little thing," Flora said. "Though I wouldn't have thought she'd be to your taste."

"Of whom are you speaking?"

"The little Lindel. Tell me, what was it? A winter tide romance with your tenant's daughter? Did you follow her to town, all a-pant like a dog on the hunt? Or was it love at first sight that made you throw me over for her?"

"Don't be vulgar, Flora."

"I? Vulgar? Surely not. I wasn't making sheep's eyes at her and in St. Paul's of all places. Nearly as bad as making such an exhibition of yourself tonight. I wouldn't myself wish to expose the young lady to such public attention."

"You don't know what you are talking about." He wouldn't justify himself to her, but every word she said made him happier to think she was no longer his lover. "If this is all you wish to say to me . . ."

"By no means. I'm not going to be made the laughingstock of London by you and some little chit just out of the schoolroom. You could have had the decency to wait a few weeks after leaving me before you began pursuing another." For an instant, a flash of something besides anger showed. Kenton thought it might be pain, if only that of wounded pride.

"No one need know I have left you," he said more gently than he thought he could.

"No one need know? Half the *ton* knows it already."

"I'm not responsible for that. No one has found a way of stopping gossip yet."

"No. I know how to use it myself, very well indeed." Her voice hardened.

"What do you mean by that?"

"Why, nothing whatever. Pursue your rural beauty if you wish. It's nothing to me." She sat back into the darkness, only the flash of jewels at wrist, throat, and earlobes giving away her position. After a moment, she gave a soft laugh as though some chance thought amused her.

"What are you planning, Flora?" Kenton asked warily.

"Nothing whatever. I hope your wooing prospers and quickly too."

"I'm not wooing anyone."

"No? That's good. You won't mind so much when she flees the town, pursued by rumors."

He knew she could do it. "Why would you even think of doing such a thing? Miss Lindel is nothing to you."

Did she shrug those white shoulders? "Everyone already believes you are in love with her. And even a blind man could tell she is in love with you."

"Don't be ridiculous. Miss Lindel feels nothing for me. We only met for the first time the other day." For an instant, his mind went back to his last afternoon at Finchley, just after the parish committee meeting, one of the few duties as lord of the manor that he enjoyed. He'd run into Miss Pike in the doorway and had looked up to see a beautiful girl. . . .

"Feels nothing?" Flora again gave her low intimate laugh. "She gazes at you as if you were her entire dependence and delight. When you smile at her, her face lights and she hangs on your words as if they were Holy Writ. A woman sees these things, Ken, even if a man can't."

"Whether she is or she isn't has nothing to do with the case. Keep your tongue between your teeth."

"Or what? You can't harm my reputation; I've none. I cannot hurt your reputation; you are too well-known. What scandal can there be in a man ten years on the town? But an innocent bud is so easily blackened by a breath of rumor. I will have no trouble convincing everyone that this innocent is nothing of the sort. She has already thrown in her lot with that Paladin creature and everyone knows what she is. If your little miss flees from town, everyone will believe you toyed with her, broke her heart, and then discarded her."

"You're a vile creature, Flora Armitage. I never knew it before now."

"A woman must take revenge however she can. Our powers are so slight compared to a man's."

Fortunately, they drew rein in front of his house before he could give in to his impulse to strangle her. "I feel no anxiety for Miss Lindel," he said as he opened the door. "I'm sure she'll enjoy her Season to the full."

"We shall see."

He left her the last word, though it went against the grain. The windows of his rooms were glowing, for he'd invited Dom to stay until his case was settled. It was pleasant to think there was someone at home with whom to discuss the night's occurrences. Yet when he opened his door, he heard more than one male voice.

"Chavez!" he exclaimed in delight, advancing to shake hands with his island agent. Of both Portuguese and German parentage, Miguel Chavez wore his brown hair a trifle long and had a luxurious mustache spreading across his upper lip. Except for these, he could have been any slightly sunburnt English gentleman fresh from a sea voyage.

"My lord. It is good to see you again."

"And you. You had a good crossing?"

"Excellent. No accidents to any of our cargo. The captain was most attentive to my wishes regarding the sea lanes."

"I can't wait to see them."

Dom unfolded his length from his chair. "If you two are going to croon over the infants, I'm going to bed."

"No, stay, Dom. Chavez, I'm not returning with you to Finchley Place. You'll have to go and see to the repotting and their care. Don't let Bledsoe walk over you. He's a good man, but a bit old-fashioned."

"Very good, my lord. But, pardon me, I thought you would be anxious to do the work yourself."

"I am but something has come up here in town."

Dom looked at him with narrowed eyes. "What is it? You look as if . . ."

"Please don't say I look as if I'm in love."

"Are you?"

"No, I don't believe so."

"Then what is it?"

"I beg your pardon, Mr. Swift," Chavez put in, his

dark eyes gleaming. "Lord Danesby looks to me as if he is preparing for battle, not for love."

"Don't tell me it's another duel," Dom said, concern creasing his brow.

"No, thank God," Kenton said. "But it is battle of a sort. There's a fair maiden in peril and a dragon to slay." He started toward his bedroom to change out of his formal attire. Glancing back into the room, he added, "Maybe two dragons."

Chapter Seven

Still wearing her ball gown of silver net over white crape, but with her hair tumbled down her back, Maris wafted down the hallway to rap lightly on Lilah's door. The house seemed very silent but a light gleamed from under the door, giving Maris hope that Lilah was still awake.

"Who is there?" Lilah asked, her voice hushed and hurried.

"Maris."

"Oh. Come in."

Already in bed, Lilah bore a writing desk across her knees. As Maris entered, she finished reading over a sheet of paper and signed her name. Then she firmly corked the ink bottle set into its own round compartment. "Take this away, will you?"

"Certainly." She moved the desk to stand on Lilah's battered bureau. It was even more tawdry than the one in her own room. Glancing about her, for she'd never been in here before, she realized that Lilah must have refused to occupy the nicer room, for the Paladins had arrived before them and so had had first choice.

"Not the most luxurious surroundings," Lilah said, noticing the turn of Maris's eyes and reading the trend of her thoughts. "But no one sees them but ourselves."

"I don't mind. No, I really don't. I know our mothers have to save what they can."

"Yes."

"It's foolish to yearn for fine things when one misses people so."

Lilah turned a most penetrating gaze on her. "You feel that, do you?"

"Naturally I miss my mother and sister."

A twist to Lilah's mouth came and went so quickly Maris couldn't be certain she'd seen it. "Naturally."

"And it isn't as though I were used to luxury, nor, for that matter, afraid of poverty," Maris said, wondering about Lilah. She wasn't more than a year or so older yet she seemed so much wiser. "We have only the little Father left and the allowance Mother receives from her family."

"You're not afraid of being poor?" Lilah asked, quite as incredulously as she would have asked a lamb if it was not afraid of the lion sleeping in its pen.

"No. Poverty means no money and we've never had very much to spare. But one can make and mend quite well and even come to enjoy it. A friend of mine, Miss Menthrip, says that it takes more intelligence to be genteelly impoverished than to be prime minister. Though, to tell the truth, I'm never quite sure how she means that."

"She has the right of it, if one considers the caliber of today's politicians." She lay back against her pillows, the long ripples of her dark gold hair spread out from under her cap. "Not to be afraid of poverty," she said softly, as if musing to herself. "To think of being poor as a game, one's wits against the world. But don't you find it diminishes your soul?"

"How could it? Most of the great figures of history had no money . . . well, the religious ones anyway. And poets, even the greatest, never have twopence to rub together."

"But to argue with butchers for credit and stave off bailiffs when run into debt . . ."

"Of course, one must live within one's means." Maris smiled. "We can hardly say we are accustomed to living in the height of decadence," she added, gingerly testing a chair before she sat on it. The one in her room always turned a leg just as she sat down.

"No, we are not spoiled. But can it be done, year after year? There may be children, droughts, crop failures . . ."

"You sound as if you have some future in mind, Lilah. What is it?"

"A man, of course."

"What man?"

"Will you be so kind as to hand me my letter?" She pointed to the lap desk. A sheet of paper, closely written over, lay on the slanted wooden top. Maris wished she hadn't been so carefully raised, for her curiosity demanded a long and hungry glance. But she kept her eyes raised and never stole so much as a peek. Yet even with the best will in the world, she couldn't help reading the salutation. 'My dearest Nehemiah . . .'"

"Nehemiah Preston has been my beau since we were children. He keeps sheep on a farm not far from Hay-on-Wye where I was born." Lilah opened the letter and added a postscript.

That explained the slight lilt in her voice, for Hay

was on the border between England and Wales. "A shepherd?"

"Yes. The farm was his father's and it came to him. At the end of the Season, I shall marry him."

Maris didn't mean to be impertinent but the words wouldn't be denied. "Won't your mother object?"

"She may if she wishes," Lilah said coolly. "It will make no difference to me. I have already delayed for two years. I won't wait any longer."

"Two years? This Season and last year's?"

"Exactly. My mother's wish has always been for me to make a dazzlingly successful marriage. She felt that my marrying Mr. Preston would be too great a comedown for a gentleman's daughter. But what of it? I despise all this emphasis on gentility and superficial appearance. I didn't not 'take' at my first appearance. I told Mother then that any further attempt would merely be a waste of money and time. Time I could use to grow accustomed to my future. But she wouldn't listen. She arranged this plan with your mother so that her costs would be less but the outcome will be the same."

Maris felt a little as though she had stood on a beach to watch the tide come in, only to be swept away by a breaker. Lilah looked quite different, her eyes sparkling with determination, her cheeks flushed with indignant rose, and her chin lifted in defiance. Her voice had a ring in it, nothing like her usual soft tones. Maris felt that it was just as well for Lilah's plans that no young men were present to see her looking so extraordinarily beautiful. She wondered if Mr. Preston appreciated the qualities of his future bride. If it were left to Lilah, he'd soon be a exceedingly prominent sheep farmer.

"Then you don't want to be in London at all?"

"No. Not even remotely. I did, however, promise Mother that I would not act in any manner calculated to give people a disgust of me." She smiled, a touch slyly. "I could have, very easily. The *ton* is so readily shocked."

"What would you have done?" Maris breathed, fascinated.

Lilah made an airy gesture. "I had so many plans to be outrageous. It's just as well I need not implement them. It would be just my misfortune to find that instead of making me an outcast, my exploits would make me the toast of town."

"That would be a risk," Maris agreed. "So instead you show no interest in gentlemen or indeed anything very much."

"Exactly. I cultivate an air of world-weariness, though I must confess I do still sometimes blush for Mother. She is so blatant about throwing me at various eligible gentlemen's heads." A cloud of memory seemed to wrap about Lilah. "I should warn you, I suppose. Mama's methods are not always suitably subtle. In fact . . ."

Maris waited, but Lilah had obviously thought the better of what she'd begun to say.

"But, come," Lilah said, smiling with genuine warmth. "You didn't knock on my door to ask about my future, did you?"

"Not really. Speaking of Mrs. Paladin, she said something to me this evening that I didn't understand."

"What was it?"

Briefly, Maris explained the circumstances of Lord Danesby escorting her to her chaperon's side. "Your mother asked me if he'd offered me a *carte blanche.* I know it means 'white card' but what the true meaning is I cannot guess."

"Are you truly as innocent as all that?" Lilah marveled. "I hadn't thought anyone was."

Though Maris felt a spark of anger at being thought such a ninnyhammer, she concealed it. She couldn't see that it was in any way her fault. Girls were brought to town to acquire "town bronze," not because they had it already. Give her a month and she'd have as good a grasp of the essentials of town life as any creature born and bred in London.

Lilah twisted a lock of her loosened hair as she thought. "How to put this delicately . . ."

"Never mind delicacy. If I am not to continually make a fool of myself, I must know these things. I can't spend my whole life so innocent that I am mistaken for ignorant."

"I quite agree. But take care with whom you speak. I don't mind; heaven knows I find a little plain-speaking refreshing. There are others, higher sticklers than Mother, who would take it ill that any young woman would be acquainted with such a phrase."

"But what does it mean?" Maris asked again, more impatiently.

"To offer a girl *carte blanche* means that a man wishes to enter into an irregular relationship with her. He offers her in effect a blank draft on his bank. Anything she wants could be hers so long as his interest does not cool."

"'Irregular relationship,'" Maris echoed, not feeling particularly enlightened.

Lilah sighed. "Love but not marriage. Do you understand?"

"No. Why wouldn't a man just marry the girl if he loved her that much?"

"Men don't always marry where they desire nor always love whom they desire. Sometimes they are married already. Sometimes they don't wish to be married or at least not to be married to a girl of much beauty but low station."

Maris shook her head at the complications people put in the way of an essentially simple matter. "It sounds very odd and most uncomfortable for everyone."

"Men don't find it so. They find it very convenient. Certainly there are many lowborn girls who choose the ducats in hand of a wealthy lover rather than let their beauty be wasted on the streets."

Putting all her confusion aside, Maris returned to her former point. "Your mother shouldn't have suggested such a thing. Lord Danesby would never . . ."

"No, I doubt he would. His reputation is not all it should be perhaps, but no one has ever said he cast out lures to unmarried girls. Too afraid of being trapped into matrimony, I would guess."

"If he doesn't interest himself in unmarried girls," Maris said, trying to fit her new knowledge into her image of Lord Danesby, "does that mean . . . ? No."

"That married women are fair game? Indeed. Last year, he and Mrs. Armitage were notorious. Of course, she's no innocent either. Her passion for Alastair Lamont two years ago was shockingly blatant. They say she was so careless that even her husband began to suspect. Then Lamont married that little American creature and Mrs. Armitage set her cap for Danesby. He never had a chance of escaping her toils. She's still quite handsome," Lilah admitted kindly, "if terribly old. She must be at least forty."

Maris, her mind whirling with new thoughts, didn't remember whether she said good night before she left. Undressing in her room, she lay her dress carefully over the back of the chair before hurrying into bed. Pulling the covers up to stay warm, she changed under the blankets. She couldn't tell if the room had suddenly grown colder or if it was just her.

"Don't be ridiculous," she scolded herself, blowing out the candle. "Did you expect him to live like a monk on a mountaintop while he was waiting for you? He's a man and the flesh is weak. It says so in Mark or maybe it is in Matthew." Her feet were too cold to carry her out of bed to check the reference.

"Mrs. Armitage?" she thought in some disgust. "She's so hardened. What on earth could he see in her?" She was rather pretty for, as Lilah said, an older woman. Perhaps she had all the seductive powers of a Salome. Certainly she was more appealing than a washed-out blond virgin who couldn't open her mouth without making some ghastly faux pas.

Maris never ceased to be amazed by how readily her own mind could put her in the wrong. Point by point it examined the sophisticated perfections of a Mrs. Armitage compared to the awkward and obviously homespun charms of a country miss. In every instance, save for youth, Maris came out the loser. After all, what good was youth? Everyone could fool her, everyone could patronize her and, with justice, everyone could and probably did laugh at her. Lord Danesby would never lower himself to think of her as a possible bride. The wisest course would be to put him right out of her thoughts.

He had been kind to her that evening. He had seemed to enjoy her conversation, though she could not now recall all that they'd discussed. She remembered him laughing at something clever she had said. His laugh, even in memory, enlivened her like a sudden ray of sun breaking through bed curtains to wake a lazy lie-a-bed. She'd been unable to resist the tug of his hand on hers as he led her away to dance.

Not even the remembrance of Mrs. Armitage's odious behavior could spoil Maris's memories of this evening. Maris puzzled over the coincidence for a moment. Mrs. Armitage had said that Maris had been making sheep's eyes at Lord Danesby but surely that had been before he'd talked to her. True, she'd been present in the cathedral but surely too far away to see Maris's expression while speaking to his lordship. Had it merely been malice that had engendered that remark? How odd that it should strike so near to the gold of truth.

She fell asleep toward dawn, still torn even in her dreams between her love for Lord Danesby and this new light on his character. She seemed to see him as a monk one moment and a libertine the next, praying in one guise, and inviting laughing women of low morals to sit on his knee in the other. Maris couldn't see herself anywhere. She certainly wasn't present in the cloister, though she watched every step Lord Danesby took. Nor could she find herself among the multitude of women thronging about him where he sat on a golden throne.

When she awoke at last, her mouth was dry and she could scarcely manage to open both eyes at the same time. The cup of hot tea that the hired maid presented did help to awaken her. By the time she came downstairs to greet Mrs. Paladin and Lilah, her spirits were rebounding. Lord Danesby had found her interesting enough to remain by her side for an hour, surely more than any other girl present last night could boast.

"Dear, dear Maris," Mrs. Paladin said. "You must come and see the tributes that were delivered this morning. Charming! If only your mother were here. Now, you must immediately write notes of thanks to all your admirers. You mustn't appear haughty or in any way vain."

"No, of course not," Maris murmured, raising up on tiptoe to see around Mrs. Paladin.

Lilah took pity on her. "She can't write notes until she sees what she's thanking them for. Mother, let her come in."

Bunches of flowers lay on the polished oak of the morning room table. Some were quite formal in design, looking, to Maris's eyes, beautiful enough for a ball. Others were loose sheaves of hyacinth or calendula or other heralds of spring. Each bore a card. By the time she sorted through them, she realized that at least six gentlemen had thought it worthwhile to send her a bouquet. "How kind everyone is," she said. "Oh, look. These are from Sir Rigby Barrington. I didn't even dance with him."

She missed Mrs. Paladin's expression, but the older woman's tone was cold. "I am well aware of that. In truth, I meant to read you something of a scold regarding your manners."

"At least she threw him over to dance with Lord Danesby, Mother," Lilah said, turning the pages of the *Gazette*.

"Kindly don't be vulgar, Lilah," Mrs. Paladin said, but perhaps her daughter's reminder of Maris's triumph softened her. "Never mind," she added. "If Sir Rigby is willing to forgive you, so am I."

Lord Danesby had not sent any flowers. She told herself she didn't care. To have danced with him, to have been the sole focus of his brilliant eyes however briefly, was more of his attention than she'd ever dreamed she'd have. Even if she should never see him again, she had enough to fuel her happiness for a lifetime. Yet, despite that, she couldn't keep a slight pang of disappointment at bay. It would have crowned her first appearance to have been able to write to Lucy that she'd received even the humblest drooping daisy from Lord Danesby.

The letter she wrote to her mother made no mention of their landlord. She also concealed behind a screen of cheerful words her growing anxiety about Mrs. Paladin. Her notions of a proper young lady's actions did not march very well with Mrs. Lindel's. Mrs. Paladin was always urging Maris to be less reserved, to show more vivacity. "Don't stand there like a sacrificial maiden, girl. Smile at the gentlemen. Flirt with your fan. Let them see your interest."

Lilah demonstrated these arts to perfection in the privacy of their rooms, yet Maris did not notice her actually using any of these techniques when evening brought about another formal affair. Though Lilah was punctiliously polite, missing none of the forms of polite society, she did not show any particular rapture at being solicited to dance. The dry wit that Maris was rapidly coming to cherish was not on view for gentlemen. Mr. Nehemiah Preston would find no rivals in London.

Waiting by her chaperon's chair, Maris noticed that, once again, many eyes seemed fixed upon her.

Considerable whispering broke out wherever she went, though neither fact seemed to daunt the gentlemen soliciting her hand for various dances. There were more than yesterday, yet Maris could not feel gratification. Some of the younger gentlemen seemed less interested in dancing with her than being seen to dance with her. There was nothing specific to put her finger on; just something in the way they looked past her, nodding and grinning at their friends off the floor.

When the stirring, staring, and whispering grew more pronounced, Maris glanced about with a frown. Looking toward the entry, she sighed blissfully. Lord Danesby had arrived.

He did not approach her for more than an hour which, as he appeared after the hostess had retired from the doorway, left Maris with some dozen dances to labor through. She tried to be pleasant to all who solicited her to dance, yet she kept one eye out for a glimpse of his dark head. She marked how he danced first with the hostess's rawboned daughter. Miss Hester Devoe's lack of beauty would place no bars to her making a high marriage, not with ten thousand pounds waiting on her majority. As for Lady Clarice Shallcross, her beauty would more than reconcile any husband to her father's fatal gambling habit. As for all the other honorables, misses, and ladies, she envied them nothing except that they danced with Lord Danesby before she did.

Yet at last, shortly after the supper interval, he appeared before her, making his bow. "No, sir," she said in answer to his query. "I am not engaged for this."

"Excellent." His smile at Mrs. Paladin was a trifle

tight as he looked to her for tacit permission. She waved her large fan and gave him an eager nod.

But Maris felt no surge of exhilaration as she had the night before while holding his hand in anticipation of the first beat of the music. He seemed far away, not smiling at her but looking rather grimly over her head. When he did smile, he looked more like an animal baring its teeth than a man reveling in amusement. His eyes were hard as he dared those who stared and whispered to meet his gaze.

In the dance, he moved like an automaton, his steps perfectly executed but without emotion. Even his fixed smile had more than a passing resemblance to the half-opened grin of a clockwork doll. Maris had always found such toys rather eerie, as though everything needful were present to create a human being except a soul.

When the dance ended, Maris sighed and said, "Thank goodness," just audibly. Lord Danesby glanced at her sharply.

"Permit me to find you some refreshment, Miss Lindel."

"That is very kind of you, my lord, but I am quite well."

"I insist."

She had not will enough where he was concerned to resist. He sat her down on a small sofa, just big enough to permit a tête-à-tête while not allowing space for a gooseberry. There were many such scattered about the big room, a conceit of their hostess.

To her surprise, he did not hurry away in search of cooling drinks. He snapped his fingers and a waiter appeared, already bearing two glasses of champagne on his silver tray. "I came prepared,"

Lord Danesby said with a bow and his first genuine smile as he handed her the glass.

She took it in her gloved hand but couldn't stop her face from scrunching up as she sipped the wine.

"You don't care for champagne?"

"Not very much," Maris admitted. "Terribly provincial of me, I know."

"Not at all." He leaned toward the waiter and exchanged two words. Then Lord Danesby sat down beside her. "We have only a few minutes to talk," he began. "I must be brief but we have much to discuss."

Maris felt an odd flutter of anticipation within her. What was this leading to? Was another of her dreams, the tenderest of them all, about to come true? "Have we?"

"Indeed, yes. Through no fault of your own, Miss Lindel, you have become involved in an intrigue."

"An intrigue?" she echoed, lost and disappointed. She'd known how impossible her dreams were yet it hurt nonetheless when they came to nothing. Then her wits came back to her. "Does this have anything to do with a certain Mrs. Armitage?"

"You've heard the rumors then?"

Maris looked down at her hands, folded in such a ladylike way in her lap. "Not all rumors are false, my lord."

He crossed his legs uneasily. "No. What have you heard?"

"That you and Mrs. Armitage were . . ." She cast about for a ladylike term.

"These are not matters with which you need concern yourself. All that is past. But she is a vindictive creature, more so than I would have believed."

"You broke with her?"

"Yes. And with considerably less tact than I might have used. I felt . . ." A dark look came into his eyes, but Maris could not tell where his loathing was focused, whether on Mrs. Armitage or upon himself. "I felt as though I were riding very fast toward a ravine and if I did not instantly turn my horse, I should be lost."

"Yes, I know what that is like," Maris murmured.

"There was no time for tact. I merely wanted to divert disaster and I have done so but I never meant any mud to touch you."

"I? I'm sure I have nothing to fear from Mrs. Armitage." Nothing except a further reference to sheep's eyes—revolting term!

"On the contrary. We both have much to fear from her vituperative tongue."

"Gossip? Why should I fear gossip? I've nothing on my conscience. I've done no wrong."

"I'm afraid in our world, Miss Lindel, that innocence is no guarantee against calumny."

"'Be thou as pure as snow, as chaste as ice . . .'" She thought it very unfair that she was both pure and chaste yet would receive no protection.

"Precisely." He smiled for the first time with that genuine warmth that never failed to steal her breath. "Isn't it amazing how Shakespeare always has the last word?"

"He shares honors with the Bible, I think."

"Yes. 'All wickedness is but little to the wickedness of a woman.'"

Maris thought for a moment. "I don't know that one."

"It's from the Apocrypha. You wouldn't know it but it's interesting."

"I'm no bluestocking, heaven knows, yet sometimes I do envy men their greater opportunities for learning. If . . . if I knew more," she said, hesitating over a new thought. "If I knew more, perhaps I'd understand why someone whom I hardly know and have never harmed . . ." She bit her lip. "Perhaps I'd know how to defend myself and, even, how to carry the war into the enemy camp."

"Would you?" He looked at her as if he'd never seen her before, not only a stranger but one to be admired. She felt she would do anything to keep that glow in Lord Danesby's eyes.

"I could show you how," he said, then bit his lip as though to recall the words. He shook his head so sharply that he disarranged his hair. He pushed it back, uncaring of his reputation as the neatest man of his generation. He felt as if he'd done more with half a dozen words to ruin her innocence than Flora Armitage had done yet.

"Forget that I spoke," he said.

"No, I cannot. If you have a plan to discomfit her, I am willing to assist you."

"I would be compounding my own villany if I did anything of the sort. It is my fault that Mrs. Armitage is angry. I shall mend what I can and hope that her native good sense returns. You have your friends to help you with whatever mud may splash on you. Is your mother returned yet from her journey?"

"Not yet. I had a letter from her today. She is still concerned about my sister's health but in her postscript Sophie says that she is well."

Realizing that she'd been beside him for far too long if she was to be safe from more gossip, Kenton stood up. "Shall I return you to your chaperon?"

"Of course," she said, smiling and gathering her

shawl about her shoulders. She was lovely when she smiled with her small dimple peeping out. It was buried in the soft corner of her rosebud pink mouth, a most kissable corner. Kenton passed his hand over his eyes. He had no business noticing such things.

Chapter Eight

By the end of the first week, Kenton's frustration with the bullheadedness of society had grown to the point where he could hardly contain himself. Even his closest cronies were met with a glare if they so far forgot themselves as to make a joke about his supposed flirt. Only Dom, of the abstracted calm, could approach the subject without receiving a savage set-down.

"Dragons proving harder to vanquish than you thought?" he asked quietly one evening when Kenton had returned home from a card party.

"Impossible. They're not dragons; they're hydras. Lop off one head and three more grow. I've tried showing an avuncular interest in the girl. The gossips reply that I'm trying to lull her suspicions of my reputation. I ignore her and I instantly become a heartless rake bent on flirtation. Can't a man and a woman exist in a peaceful state of neither love nor hate? Can't they be friends?"

"They can, I suppose. I have never met such a pair, but then I am not widely traveled."

Kenton dropped wearily into a chair. "If it weren't a coward's part, I should go home. But I cannot allow Miss Lindel to face this alone."

"Surely they would soon forget?"

"Not they," Kenton said with a snort. "I'm afraid this has already gone too far to permit her to continue without fingers continually being pointed at her. Poor thing. It's none of her fault."

"I do have a suggestion."

"Go ahead. I'd take a recommendation from the devil himself at this point."

"I'm not quite so cunning as that."

A hint of wariness in his friend's tone made Kenton raise his eyes from their contemplation of the hearth rug. "Well, go on. I promise to keep my temper."

"That's something at any rate. My plan is that you return to Mrs. Armitage."

"As a lover? I'd dance with the devil first. She's shown me her true nature—mercenary, vindictive, cruel."

"Are you so surprised by it? Come, Ken, don't play the innocent. You knew what she was when you began. A married woman allowed to run her length by an indulgent, stupid husband and a world that will let a woman commit any folly so long as she is reasonably discreet."

"You wrong the world, Dom. She is not received everywhere."

"Are you?"

"As a rule, yes. I am an eligible gentleman, no matter what follies I may have committed. So long as there is some hope that I shall marry one of their daughters, the marriage-minded mamas will never desert me."

"And when you marry, will all evils be forgotten?"

"It's not fair, no. A man may sow wild oats as he will before he is married. But that is the way of the world."

"When Miss Lindel marries, will her unfortunate entanglement in your romantic affairs be forgotten?"

"I imagine so. I doubt anyone believes in their heart of hearts that Miss Lindel is a Jezebel. One need only look into her eyes. Her eyes are very clearly those of an innocent and unspoiled girl."

Dom steepled his fingers in front of his nose. "Then, logically, the answer to your difficulty is to marry Miss Lindel yourself. Both your reputations will be mended and your former inamorata will be left with nothing to say that will interest even the worst gossip in London. You will, in effect, have spiked her guns."

"Marry Miss Lindel? Oh, don't be ridiculous, Dom. She's just a snip of a girl, hardly fledged yet."

"You've not done so well wooing more mature charmers," Dom said pitilessly. "Besides, I haven't liked to mention it but I've noticed a certain cynicism growing in you since we left school. These mercenary affairs may have convenience to recommend them yet I cannot choose but to think they are damaging to the soul."

"Return to your sermons, Father," Kenton said, tossing a book at his tall friend. Without disturbing himself, Dom caught it, glanced at the fly leaf, and began to read it. He was comfortably set for hours. Kenton found no such peace. At last he went out again, though he'd previously refused with thanks the invitation to a cotillion ball.

"He never took his eyes from you the entire evening!" Mrs. Paladin said, rejoicing. "Oh, nothing was ever more certain than this."

Maris turned carefully away from the mirror, the huge circle of her hoops swaying broadly. "More certain than what, ma'am?

"Why, what else?" She lowered her voice to a whisper. "Lord Danesby's head over ears in love with you."

"Mother," Lilah said warningly from the floor. She had taken the pins out of her mouth when Maris moved.

"You may say what you choose, Lilah, but you will look nohow when dearest Maris is 'my lady.'"

The hired maid came to the door before Lilah could make the sharp reply Maris could all but see trembling on her lips. "Beg pardon, Mrs. Paladin," she said. "Lady Osbourne has called."

"Lady Osbourne? Heavens and me with my skirt all over snips!" Brushing at herself, she hurried out.

"Turn this way again, Maris," Lilah said. "This skirt needs another breadth turned up or you'll trip when you make your curtsy to the Queen."

"I still cannot thank you enough for offering me the use of your presentation gown."

"Pish. I shan't use it again. A few new trimmings and lace and no one will know it ever appeared before."

"It does seem a monstrous waste that so elegant a dress should only have one airing." Maris looked over Lilah's head into the pier glass. The wide, wide skirt narrowed abruptly to a fashionable body, trimmed over the shoulders with ribbon. She grinned at the remarkable picture she presented. "It's enough to throw one into whoops when you collect that our grandmothers wore such things every day of their lives."

"The hard part is learning to walk in them with

any kind of elegance. One stumble and you lie on the ground with your hoop belling over you. I wore three petticoats when I was presented."

"I only pray there's no wind. With this hoop and a headful of feathers, I would go sailing down the street like a full-rigged ship."

They giggled like sisters over that ridiculous picture. Lilah reached up to tap Maris's hand. "I will say that in one respect I enjoyed this Season far more than my last. I am glad that I could share it with you."

This tribute from the intensely reserved Lilah brought unaccustomed tears into Maris's eyes. "I shouldn't have been able to bear it if it hadn't been for you. All this talk . . ."

"Yes," Lilah said, retreating as was her wont from too much notice. "Turn about or this hem will never be straight."

The vast silken overskirt was at last pinned to Lilah's satisfaction and Maris was stepping out of it before Mrs. Paladin returned. If she had been in alt before, her excitement now reached into the clouds. "Mercy, I could almost ask you to prick me with one of your pins, Lilah, for I am in such a state I hardly know whether I am awake or asleep. You'll never guess what Lady Osbourne came to offer."

They did not need to ask, for her explanation came with the next breath. "An invitation to visit her country home . . . one of the showplaces of the country! Her third daughter is to make her presentation at the same Drawing Room as you, Maris. You, it seems, made a great hit with her at some party or other."

"What is her name, ma'am?"

"Oh, mercy, I don't . . . Cloris, or some such."

"I didn't know she was Lady Osbourne's daughter. We were talking of the trial our parents inflicted on us by giving us such names as must give rise to comment." Maris did not mention that Lilah had taken part in this conversation as well.

Mrs. Paladin took no notice of this interjection. "She further said that she had no opinion of ill-natured persons who play hob with the good names of young ladies which I thought most delicate. Such an opportunity for you two to make close friends with the future mothers of England."

"I hardly think Lady Osbourne meant to include me in her flattering offer, Mother."

"Hush, Lilah. Of course she did. How may I go to chaperon our dear Maris if you don't come, too?"

"But I hardly need to make close friends with, as you say, the future of England."

"You never can be certain," Mrs. Paladin said with a lofty air of mystery. "You may yet have daughters of your own to establish creditably in the world. Maintaining those acquaintances through the years may serve them, if not yourself. Why, if I had not kept up a correspondence with Mrs. Lindel, I should not now have the pleasure of her daughter's companionship. What a grief that would have been."

Perhaps, Maris thought, the worldliness of London was beginning to infect her thoughts. Why else would she be so inwardly certain that it was not her companionship that Mrs. Paladin appreciated so much as the invitation Maris had netted. She sighed. "When are we to go?"

Three days later, after the nerve-wracking ordeal of a presentation to a weary-looking queen, Maris relaxed against the dusty squabs of a hired chaise.

Her head still ached from the weight of the feathers and she felt certain that the dent she could feel under her hair would never fill in. Nevertheless, it had been one of the high points of her life. She could imagine herself in thirty years regaling her grandchildren with her impressions of Queen Charlotte. She had been gracious and grandmotherly, nodding regally as each young lady approached and sank. Her response to the quickly becoming notorious Miss Lindel had been no less so. Maris herself had been blushing from the toes upward all the while.

"I wish," she said idly, "that one of these clever people would find some way for a memory to be frozen forever."

"A memory?" Lilah echoed.

"Yes. Some way that I could show my mother all that happened today. What I looked like, each step I took toward the queen, a memory frozen for all time."

"Preposterous!" Mrs. Paladin said from her corner.

Lilah patted Maris's hand. "We shall dress you again when your mother returns. Even the jewels, if we can borrow them for an hour one morning."

Because it would have been a disaster not to adorn oneself for such an occasion, Mrs. Paladin had rented a very fine copy of an elegant parure. Draped in a necklace of fish-scale pearls and sparkling paste with matching bracelets, fully three inches wide, and chandelier earrings tied on with pink silk, Maris had been the equal of any other girl, to the eye at least. Some of them, Lilah had assured her, even those with the longest lineages, were wearing jewelry just as simulated as her own.

"I hope we may," Maris said. "I would love for Mother to see the entire array." Tucked into her elegant bodice, more dear than even real jewels would have been, was a letter from Mrs. Lindel, wishing her daughter every success and informing her of her immense pride in Maris's accomplishments. That her duty to one daughter upon Sophie's relapse had kept her from this great event would be, she said, not a grief but a regret. Maris had written at once that nothing in the world was more important than Sophie's recovery. If that required Mrs. Lindel's presence, then she would not feel even regret.

"When you marry," Mrs. Paladin said, "you may have your portrait painted in your wedding gown and I'm certain your husband will bestow the family jewels upon you. I have heard a tale that the Danesbys still possess a great many Elizabethan and even medieval jewels. The present viscount's ancestors were famous dandies, you know. If that is what they called them then," she added, pondering historical realities. "At any rate, men wore a great many more jewels even than women in those days."

"I have heard similar stories," Maris said, ignoring the implications in this speech. "But no one in Finchley believes them."

As they went south, the crowded streets of London became ever busier until fading out at last into rural beauty. Maris begged to have the windows down. She breathed in what felt like her first lungful of clean air in weeks. But Mrs. Paladin fetched out her handkerchief and complained of the dust, so up went the windows. One stuck, rather, and Maris thought Mrs. Paladin would die of an apoplexy brought on by coughing. Yet, because it had rained the day before, there was actually very little dust. The fields looked like velvet in a dozen shades of green.

Durham House commanded respect by size alone, for certainly architectural merit had passed it by. Bits of it were brick, quite a lot of it was half timbered, one wing comprised the Palladian ideal while attempting, like a grand dame come down in the world, to ignore the questionable neighbor in early English attire across the way. A history of England in stone, the great house snaked and twisted like a dragon across the acres.

In the vestibule their hostess met them amid masses of deep oak woodwork relieved with cream marble, veined with chocolate. After greeting them, Lady Osbourne escorted them to their rooms herself. "We began holding a house party after the Drawing Room when my first gel was presented. She's Mrs. Holdenough now, though we have hopes of dear Robert being mentioned in the next Honor's List. They, alas, are still in Lisbon."

Mrs. Paladin hung upon her hostess's every utterance as though her words held the key to salvation. She expressed herself delighted with everything, from her north-facing room to the view over the stable yard. Maris felt that Mrs. Paladin wouldn't have objected if her room had been *in* the stable so long as her hostess bore a title.

"Please notice, my dears, this little plan of the house." Lady Osbourne picked up a piece of paper from the topmost pillow on the bed. "We have thirty-two bedrooms here spread over all three floors. Even frequent visitors can become lost so I had my secretary draw these. It seemed the most sensible solution to the difficulty of people wandering in an hour late to dinner."

Looking at Lady Osbourne's plump, red, and confident face, Maris had no doubt that this plan was indeed the most rational and efficient system. She would not have permitted anything less.

"Oh, I don't need that," Mrs. Paladin said. "I'm sure I could never forget after the marvelous times I had here last Season."

"No one ever believes they'll need a map," Lady Osbourne said patiently. "But every year someone invariably loses himself. Even Lord Osbourne has been known to become confused and he was born in this house. Keep the map in your reticule, dear Mrs. Paladin, just to humor a hostess."

"The girls and I will be happy to obey you. Yes, girls?"

"Of course."

Leaving Mrs. Paladin to rest after the journey, Lady Osbourne deigned to explain the strange floor plan of her home. "Partly it is the fault of Lord Osbourne's family. Every one of them wished to leave a mark on the house. Later, if you wish, you may see the banqueting hall which is confidently believed to be from the original castle built in the twelfth century. The interior, however, is pure Henry the Eighth. The only finer one in England is at Hampton Court."

Lilah's room was across the hall from her mother's and next door to Maris's. "How charming," Lilah said, moved by the Chinoserie hangings and wallpaper. Her wink at Maris told her how much Lilah appreciated the difference between this elegantly and cohesively furnished room and the bits and pieces, odds and ends decor of their rented home.

"You said the house is only partly the fault of your husband's ancestors," Maris prompted her ladyship.

"Ah, yes. The rest is the fault of his grandmother. A dear woman but she carried her vaunted eccentricity too far. She believed that so long as she continued to add to Durham House she would never die. Folly. Though, to be fair, she did live to one hundred and three according to the parish records. Fortunately, she died before she could bankrupt us entirely."

Lady Osbourne lingered in the doorway while Maris looked about her own quarters. The calm blue and white toile was soothing and the tester bed had a mattress deep enough for any fairy tale. "I hope, my dear Miss Lindel, that I am not overstepping the bounds of courtesy if I make mention of an unpleasant fact."

"This is your home, Lady Osbourne. You need not apologize for anything you say here, surely?"

The older woman nodded at Maris with a glint of favor. "Cloris approved of you. She is the highest stickler for propriety I have ever known—how she came to be my child is a mystery. Perhaps it is this age in which we live. When I was a girl, plain-speaking was the order of the day."

"I trust honesty will always have a place. What fact is it that you wish to mention, ma'am?"

Lady Osbourne came in and closed the door firmly behind her. She was not a slim person and the straight-falling folds of her pale orange robe did little for her figure. Her once-red hair showed streaks of white, though she did not seem older than Mrs. Paladin. "You are gossiped about, child.

People are saying things that, now that I look closely at you, cannot be true. Yet, such is the way of the world, that most people will believe what they hear."

Feeling her cheeks grow warm, Maris neverthe-less looked her hostess in the eyes. "I know there is some sort of story making the rounds but I do not know what it is. Mrs. Paladin says I should take no notice."

"Elvira Paladin is the most single-minded crea-ture alive. She all but ruined her own daughter's chances last year by her stubborn refusal to see the facts when they do not fit with her desires. She was like that even as a girl and it saddens me to learn that she has not changed."

"You knew her when she was a girl?"

"Yes, my dear. And your mother as well. I'm sorry to hear that your younger sister remains in indiffer-ent health." Lady Osbourne stood smiling at her with increased warmth.

"How do you . . . then it was not for Cloris's sake that you invited me?"

"Partially, partially. As I say, I respect Cloris's opin-ion when it comes to other girls. You are all, I beg your pardon, very much alike to me much in the way that one puppy is very like another save to the eye of love. I hoped very much that your mother would be able to accept my invitation for this evening but she wrote to me that it was quite im-possible and asked me to invite Elvira instead."

"You wrote to her in Yorkshire?"

"It's not the moon, child. She further asked me to take her part in explaining the circumstances in which you find yourself."

"She knows about that? She hasn't written to me about it and I . . ."

"You didn't wish to trouble her? It was kindly thought of but folly. Children cannot shelter their parents from the harshness of the world for it is always far too late by the time they begin. Sit down, Maris. I can't imagine why we are standing here in this ridiculous way."

When Lady Osbourne had informed Maris of what was being whispered about her, she sat back in shock, hot moisture springing into her eyes. "It's so unfair," she said, her voice shaking. "I never did . . . I never could! Oh, it is unconscionable. And to say such things about Lord Danesby . . . always so kind, so much the gentleman."

"He showed a severe lack of tact when he turned off Flora Armitage. One would have expected better from a man of his address. I do not care for her myself—a very immoral character—but I confess I felt some pity for her. That, naturally, was at an end the moment she dragged you into this miserable affair."

"Lord Danesby himself acknowledged that he handled her badly, ma'am."

Lady Osbourne's sandy brows rose to incredulous heights. "You have discussed this matter with Lord Danesby himself? When? Where?"

Maris soon put Lady Osbourne in possession of everything that had happened. Every meeting with Lord Danesby, from St. Paul's onward, was discussed in detail. Lady Osbourne steepled her forefingers and pressed them to her lips when asked for her advice. "I had no notion your friendship had progressed so far."

"It is nothing more than friendship, ma'am. If so much."

"I see. Well, if he has run mad, which is the other

explanation that leaps to mind, at least I have very many sturdy footmen to place him under restraint."

"Ma'am? Do you mean he is to be one of your guests?"

"Of course. He has attended every one of my little house parties. He and my son were army-mad schoolboys together. He even calls me 'Aunt.' I hoped at one time that he and my second daughter might do for one another but no man existed for her except the Reverend Mr. Ingilby. He is now serving in Canterbury and we have high hopes for his preferment." She waved that digression aside. "Why do you look so distressed, my dear?"

"I'm not," Maris began but couldn't meet Lady Osbourne's kind but slightly protruding blue eyes.

Lady Osbourne waited, her head to one side. She reminded Maris of a plump and wily robin anticipating the appearance of a furtive worm. Maris gathered courage and prepared to stick her neck out.

"I don't wish for either Lord Danesby's reputation or my own to suffer any further damage. To have both of us staying together at your home will surely raise more of a dust than even at present."

"On the contrary. It is well known that I do not countenance any form of wicked nonsense under my roof. Only if I were entirely convinced of your innocence would I have invited you here. I have made a point of mentioning to my friends that I have done so. You are as safe here, as you would be in your own mother's home."

Maris could only say that Lady Osbourne's kindness quite overwhelmed her.

But Lady Osbourne, mother of four girls, had a keener eye than Mrs. Lindel. Maris could not imagine her falling into the sort of absentminded reveries that were her own mother's habit.

Even as it seemed inevitable that Lady Osbourne would ask more probing questions, a maid entered, followed by a footman with Maris's luggage. She did not seem surprised to see her mistress there. Maris realized that the staff of a great lady must always know her precise location, if only to stay out of her way. "Mr. Breezes's compliments, my lady, and the Delacortes are arriving. Miss Dalton begs a moment of your time in the nursery as well."

"Thank you, Harbell."

The maid dipped her knees in acknowledgement. Taking no further notice of her mistress, she directed the footman where to put the bags.

"Harbell will look after you, Miss Lindel," she said, rising. "Oh, and if you should forget your map, the servants all carry one. You have only to ask."

Before she left, however, she turned that nearly clairvoyant mother's gaze on Maris once more. "Are you quite sure there's nothing further you'd like to say to me?"

Maris felt that here was someone who would understand if she said without roundaboutation, "I've been in love with Lord Danesby half my life." The impulse was strong. However, between the maid's prescence, however oblivious, and the calls on her ladyship's time, the impulse withered. "No, my lady."

"Well, then. Try not to worry too much. These things blow over quickly, leaving no trace behind them."

Maris realized that Lady Osbourne probably would have said the same thing if she had confided her attachment to Lord Danesby. "These things blow over," she reminded herself. Already the ideal image she'd cherished for so long was superseded by the reality of a mortal man prone to the same errors in judgment as the rest of fallible humanity. Lord Danesby was no nobler under the press of circumstances than any other harrassed and confused male.

Chapter Nine

As Lady Osbourne had predicted, the young ladies of the party were much too excited by the events of the day to consider going to sleep anything but tame. There was much giggling as slippered maidens stole between one room and the next. A surreptitious feast was delivered by a yawning and grinning footman under the direction of a falsely stern nanny.

Though there were only eight young ladies, they made enough noise for forty. They giggled over their presentation gowns, their beaus ideal, the offers they'd received or believed they were sure to be receiving as soon as someone stopped being so unreasonable! One girl said she knew a clever way to make a delectable dessert of the macaroons and chocolate on the tray by toasting them at her bedroom fireplace, so they began to do that at once, while two others, complete with guitar, began to sing popular songs.

For the first time in weeks, Maris could relax and feel accepted by her peers. Just at first, there'd been some whispering and a fatally loud query of "Isn't that the Lindel girl?" but when Maris showed no reaction, her pleased smile firm, her back straight, this embarrassment soon passed. Her hostesses,

Cloris and her next sister in age, could not have been more generous, insisting that Maris sit beside them. It was quite the most pleasant evening she'd spent since her arrival in town.

Lilah started to yawn at about one o'clock and excused herself. When Maris tried to go with her, feeling that two were less likely to get lost in this warren than one, Cloris would not let her go. "No, no. You must stay. We're going to be dressing Alameria's hair. I'm convinced that simple braids all around her head will suit her much more than those curls *à la Grecque* her dresser insists upon. They are far too old for her."

Flattered, Maris stayed. After a short time, Lilah reappeared and tried to draw Maris to one side. "The most appalling thing has happened," she murmured, but not quite quietly enough to escape notice.

"What's amiss?" Cloris demanded.

"Nothing. I spilled a bottle of scent in my room and now it reeks to heaven. I left the maid cleaning the carpet but now I cannot sleep in there."

"You may share my room," Maris said at once.

"Yes, that's the answer." Cloris possessed much the same decisiveness as her mother. "But dear Maris will stay with me. I have two beds in my room because my sister used to share it with me."

So it was settled with a shrug and a nod. Lilah left the party again, map in hand. "You are too kind," Maris said to Cloris.

"Nonsense. We shall be bosom friends, I hope."

But when they were alone, Cloris only wanted to talk about Lord Danesby. "Is it true you live in the same town?"

"It hardly deserves the name of town. It is more

of a village. One church, one school, one shop. Yet it is a dear place to my heart."

Cloris took no notice of Maris's modesty. "You must have met him often before you came to town."

"I'd never met him to speak to him. He keeps largely to himself when he is in Finchley, which isn't often."

"One hears so many stories," Cloris said with an artificial laugh. "I know my parents consider him almost like one of the family but I have never had much to do with him. Mama believes in keeping the nursery girls strictly segregated from strange men's society. One of her aunts made a runaway marriage when she was underage, you know." Maris shook her head wonderingly when Cloris dropped her voice to declare dramatically, "He was an escaped Jacobite."

"How thrilling! However did they meet?"

But Cloris wasn't interested in *giving* information. By the time her interrogator dropped off to sleep, Maris felt wrung dry of information about Lord Danesby. Sensitive to the presence of her own emotions in others, she guessed that here was another victim of his lordship's unconscious charm.

She actually knew very little about him and what she'd learned firsthand she managed to conceal through motives of prudence. It was obvious she'd disappointed her new "bosom friend." But greater mischief was waiting.

Cloris snored.

No ladylike sniffs or snorts issued from her bed but great hurricanes and typhoons. It started with a low rumble in her throat, which made Maris look to the window in fear of a thunderstorm. Then a snorting, growling, slurping sound arose, reminiscent of

eager tigers hunting through a muddy jungle. Then
there came, as breath blew out between her slack
lips, a rolling tympanic chord that would have
frightened the French into thinking that the entire
Scots Brigade, drums, bagpipes and all, were charg-
ing down upon them.

Maris clapped her hand over her mouth as an all-
but uncontrollable giggle started. She lay, her white
bed shaking to her laughter, and immediately realized that she'd far rather breathe scent all night
than remain with Cloris. A smell could be dissipated
by an open window but only by throwing a pillow
over Cloris's head could this snoring be tolerated.

She gathered up her clothing, but she could not
dress in the dark in the complicated finery of an
evening dress. Fortunately, Cloris had lent her a
dressing gown as well as a bed gown so that she
need not steal through the halls of Durham House
quite undressed. She pushed her feet into her
flimsy pumps and stole from the room. For an instant she paused, as Cloris's blustery breathing
halted, choked, and resumed.

Thanks to the multiplicity of windows in this, the
Stuart part of the house, Maris did not need a candle. The moon shone in with enough strength to
make even the spidery writing on the map clear.
She needed it, having taken a wrong turn somewhere between the early and late Stuart periods.

The house was deeply silent, yet every now and
then, especially near a staircase, she would hear a
distant sound of voices, too far-off to be understood.
Once, she could have sworn she heard a chorus of
singing, rather dim and faraway, yet giving an impression of boisteriousness. Somewhere a few
choice spirits were making a night of it. Though

glad that someone else was awake in the vast house, Maris thought she would be wise to avoid that company.

Passing through another endless hall, she heard snoring the equal of Cloris's and she wondered, stifling another giggle, if the man was single. Surely here was Cloris's ideal mate. Why ruin the sleep of two innocent people when they could marry each other? Of course, the plaster on their bedroom ceiling would probably collapse.

After what seemed an eternity, Maris finally recognized a bronze nymph shyly offering a bowl of fruit that stood at the entrance to her own hall. Now more tired than even before, Maris dragged herself toward the sanctuary of her bedchamber. It didn't matter if the room stank of worse things than Lilah's lavender scent. All she wanted now was a bed, or even a reasonably flat surface, and quiet.

"Miss?" someone called from behind her. Wearily, she turned about to find that same sturdy footman, holding high a branch of candles. An empty birdcage dangled from his other hand. "Are you lost, miss? And no wonder if you are, such a place as I never saw."

"No, thank you." Maris remembered to be polite. "My room is just here."

"I'll light your way, then."

"Thank you. I beg your pardon," Maris said on an afterthought. "I thought I heard . . . are there still people awake downstairs?"

His impudent grin flashed. "That there are. The young master'll sleep all day tomorrow and so will most of the others. You young ladies will have to do without 'em till nuncheon."

"I doubt many of us will be awake any earlier."

They reached her door at last. "Good night." She was far too tired to ask about the birdcage. She noticed with vague relief that there were no birds in it.

"Good night to you."

He held up his branch of candles just far enough so that she could see a foot beyond the open door. She noticed that Lilah had left a candle burning in her room and so dismissed the footman.

Hardly had she stepped on her own carpet than she realized that the light flowed over the gleaming naked chest of Lord Danesby, standing beside the bed, his fine linen shirt in his hand. "Miss Lindel?" he said, pure shock turning his voice husky.

Maris closed the door. "You know," she said, a laugh trembling in her throat, "when I saw a similar scene on the stage last week, I thought it highly improbable."

He raised his arms to pull his shirt over his head once again. Maris glanced away in haste but she noticed that the shirt was marred. It had a thin red stain over the heart. His voice, though muffled by the folds of the shirt, could still demand a response. "What are you doing here?"

Maris felt surprise but no embarrassment at having him in her room. She couldn't very well start screaming after they'd already exchanged civilities.

"I was warned that one could easily become confused in this house. Are you certain you did not lose your way, my lord?"

"On the contrary, I think it is you who are lost, Miss Lindel. And what, may I ask, are you doing wandering the halls at this hour?"

She could not betray Cloris's secret. "I don't believe that is any of your concern," she said, raising her chin defiantly.

"You made it my business when you walked through that door."

"But this is my room."

"No, it's mine." He picked his black coat from the bed and felt in the pockets. "Look. My room is clearly marked on this map."

Perforce, she took the paper he flourished at her. It was the work of an instant to compare it with her own, still showing her former room. They were cheek by jowl. "But I'm certain . . ." The lingering fragrance in the air gave her an argument. "Miss Paladin spilled that scent earlier this evening. Surely you don't use it?"

"No."

"Well, then. Does this look like the room you were shown to when you arrived?"

His breath smelled slightly of alcohol but he didn't seem at all off balance. "I didn't see it. I arrived only a few moments before dinner was to commence. Fortunately, I had planned to arrive then and journeyed down in my evening attire."

"Then who gave you this?"

"The butler."

They stood close together, puzzling out the mystery. "It's a well-run household," Maris said. "Though I suppose mistakes happen even here."

"I've often been a guest here and nothing of the sort has ever happened before. Don't distress yourself." He brushed her cheek gently with the backs of his fingers, pushing a loosened lock of hair over her shoulder. "I'll go at once."

She caught his sleeve. "Where will you sleep?"

"I'll return to the youngsters downstairs. They'll be up for hours yet. If I grow too weary for cards and dice, for I'm no heedless youth anymore, there are sofas and rugs enough to house an army in luxury."

Maris was about to offer to leave him in possession of the bedroom—Lilah could share with her if she couldn't bear a return to Cloris—when the bedroom door flew open.

"Aha!" Mrs. Paladin said, pointing a sharp finger at the surprised couple. "As I thought!"

Kenton instinctively interposed his body between Maris and the door. Nothing could be more innocent or appear more damaging than his presence in Maris Lindel's bedchamber. As though he walked through a picture gallery of Mr. Hogarth's satirical sketches, he could see small images of the inevitable consequences—threatened scandal, a forced proposal, a quick and quiet wedding, and all the misery of marriage to an incompatible woman.

Yet, like a gleam of light striking the last picture, he could believe that there were worse fates in the world than marriage to Miss Lindel. He wondered if Maris liked roses and how she would feel about traveling the world. As a companion, her viewpoint would be, he felt certain, unique.

Mrs. Paladin's shrilling broke in on his thoughts. "Little did I think that you would sink so low, my lord, as to seduce an innocent girl under this of all roofs!"

"Don't be absurd," he said coldly. "This is the last place I would have chosen." He heard Maris give a snort of muffled laughter from behind him and tried to stifle his answering smile.

"How can you stand there and grin at me? Are you entirely dead to shame, sir? You must do right by her. Thank God she has a devoted mother to look out for her interests!"

Already doors were opening in the hall. Kenton thought wryly that it was to Mrs. Paladin's advantage to have as many witnesses as possible to the theatrical storm she was brewing. They were unnecessary, however. He had every intention of settling the situation in the only honorable fashion, even though the scandal was none of his doing. He began to wonder whose doing it was.

"Mother?"

Mrs. Paladin broke off her tirade between one syllable and the next as Lilah emerged from her bedroom to stand, rubbing her eyes, beside her. At nearly the same instant, Maris stepped out from behind the shelter of Kenton's shoulder. The stunned widening of Mrs. Paladin's eyes, the way she pressed her hand to her heart as she stepped back, told him that she'd had no notion the girls had changed rooms.

The slight catch in Maris's breathing told Kenton that she, too, had caught the subtleties of the situation. He put his hand to his pocket. The only time he'd seen Mrs. Paladin had been when the entire party had crowded onto a portico at the back of the house to watch the pyrotechnics in honor of Cloris Osbourne's presentation to the Queen. It would have been an easy matter to abstract one map from his pocket and slip in another. One wouldn't even need to be a particularly good pickpocket.

He'd been distracted both by the fireworks and by the perceived necessity to avoid Maris's company. He'd bowed politely when they passed each other, but had made no attempt to single her out, though he was most impatient to hear her view of the drawing room.

If Mrs. Paladin had a guilty conscience, she made

a splendid recovery. "What will your mother say? She left you in my charge. I feel I have failed her."

Other faces were peering at them around the door frame now, other guests, a servant or two. Some looked shocked, some titillated, pointing and whispering. A few even appeared to be envious. Kenton knew they must present a very pointed moral lesson—Illicit Lovers Discovered or something of that ilk. Maris wore a simple dressing gown of golden yellow wool, her honey-colored hair shading into it where it lay loose and waving over her shoulders, pouring down from beneath a rakishly tilted cap.

"Mrs. Paladin," she began, embarking on an explanation that would be useless.

He interrupted. "We'd do better to discuss this matter privately. If you'll enter, Mrs. Paladin?"

"I also," Lilah said, crossing the lapels of her own dressing gown high on her chest. "This concerns me a little, too."

"Indeed." For the rest, he waited until the two Paladins were within and then firmly closed the door in the other guests' faces. Then he turned to face the women, his arms crossed on his chest. "Well, now . . ."

"Mother, how could you? This is going too far," Lilah proclaimed, evidently understanding her mother's perfidy at first glance. "Are you so unalterably opposed to my marrying Mr. Preston that you must drag his lordship in to stop it?"

"Who is Mr. Preston?" Kenton asked.

Raising her voice to be heard over Mrs. Paladin swearing violently that she was pure in heart, Maris explained, "I have no doubt that he is a most amiable and determined man for Lilah could have accepted nothing less in her mate."

"I don't know. I've known some clever women make a bad bargain when they marry."

"Not Lilah. She knows what she wants. She'll get it, too, mark my words."

"I confess my anxiety at this moment is not for Miss Paladin's future, but yours."

"Mine? Don't worry over that. I don't."

"You should."

Mrs. Paladin turned to him again. "You must do right by Maris, my lord. Isn't it enough that you and Mrs. Armitage between you have already sullied her name that you must break into her room as well?"

To Kenton's ears, her protestations echoed of the stage. He wondered if she took her dialogue from the same play Maris had said she'd seen.

Despite his distaste for her histrionics, he knew he was in duty bound to offer for Maris, no matter whose machinations had brought them together. He turned toward her, finding her looking at him, her lips shut tight as though upon hasty words.

"My dear Miss Lindel," he began. "Maris . . ."

Hard upon a knock, the door opened. Lady Osbourne, followed by her insignificant lord, strode in. "What is the meaning of this?"

Mrs. Paladin began to explain, only to be fixed like an insect on a pin by Lady Osbourne's powerful gaze. "Are you pitching this tarariddle, Elvira? What nonsense!"

Lord Osbourne added, "Indeed."

"No one need to have known anything about this matter if you had not seen fit to start screeching the house down. Or was that your intention? Did you mean to create as much scandal as possible? It seems hard on Miss Lindel that she should suffer for your ambition."

"This was my room," Lilah said. "Mother didn't know we'd exchanged as it happened after she retired."

"Ah, that explains it. I didn't imagine that Elvira possessed so much altruism that she'd give Danesby's fortune to Miss Lindel rather than to her own flesh and blood."

"By all means, say what you choose about me, Julia, just as though I had no ears."

"Pish," Lady Osbourne returned. "I'm not such a fool that I cannot see what is behind this pretty scene. Danesby's morals may not be all one could wish but I believe he has enough respect for me not to plan seductions under my roof."

Lord Osbourne intoned, "Indeed."

"Thank you, Aunt Julia. You have my leave to say what you choose about me."

"You are at least a gentleman, Danesby, not a counterjumper or a once-a-week beau. There are some things a gentleman does not stoop to. Seducing young ladies of good family is surely one of them."

"Thank you, Aunt Julia."

"Then I needn't marry him," Maris said, speaking for the first time."

"Not marry him?" Lady Osbourne said incredulously. "Of course you must marry him, and at once."

"Indeed," Lord Osbourne said, not unkindly.

"I shall send to Doctor's Commons for a special license at once. I wonder when they are open. If all goes well, you can be married before we all go back to town."

Turning his back on them, as the three older people began to discuss the hows and wherefores of this hasty marriage, Kenton took Maris's hands in his own. They moved to clasp his, trembling, though her eyes were calm enough.

"It must be," he said, so softly that he didn't believe even Miss Paladin, standing near, could hear him. "I offer you the protection of my name and the tenderness of my high regard. You need never fear that I will demand from you anything that you are not willing to give freely."

She gazed up at him with those wide eyes, so filled with the sweetness of dreams. In that instant, Kenton realized that Flora Armitage's guess had been right. Maris was in love with him. He hardly had time to understand this and to try to assimilate it when she blinked, her gaze hardening as it met his.

"No."

They'd been railing at her for half an hour, even Lord Osbourne managing a sentence of two words. They all had different reasons for their insistence, yet returned again and again to her utter ruination if she went from Durham House as an unmarried girl. She only shook her head, unable to take back her refusal or even to soften it.

Lord Danesby said nothing, only watching them from a window seat, his blue-sleeved arms crossed over his chest and his cravat hanging loose around his neck. She could not tell from his expression what he was thinking. Maris tried not to look at him for fear her resolve would weaken.

"No," she said again. "I am very grateful to his

lordship. However, I hardly feel that this accident, if I may call it so, needs such a drastic remedy as marriage. Do people have such a low opinion of his lordship or of me—yes, of me—to believe that we would do anything the least bit improper? You may call your own footman as a witness, Lady Osbourne. I was in this room not more than five minutes before Mrs. Paladin appeared."

"When I heard the door shut for the second time I feared something was amiss," Mrs. Paladin said.

"So your ears were on the prick?" Lady Osbourne said with a scoffing snort. "As I thought."

"The second time?" Lord Danesby asked.

"When the door closed the first time, I assumed Lilah had returned at last to her own room. When I heard it again, I knew she could not be alone. I went to her at once to see what was amiss. I did not realize that she'd given her room to Maris," she said in a sharply disillusioned tone. Maris realized that having a daughter married to the wealthy and fashionable Lord Danesby would have been both a feather in her cap and a bird in the hand. She need never fear poverty or debtors' prison with such a son-in-law. Now all this had come to nothing because her daughter had spilled scent, forcing her to give up her room.

Mrs. Paladin threw one last argument forward. "Think of your mother. Think of what your father would say."

Maris laughed. Kenton leaned forward, his elbows coming to rest on his knees. He felt the bands of steel around his heart unlatch, giving him his first full breath in what seemed like days.

"My father?" Maris said. She put aside Lilah's supporting arm, patting her hand in gratitude be-

fore standing alone in front of three disapproving
faces. Kenton watched in admiration, giving her her
moment.

"My father would have told me to stop being such
a damned fool. I will not sell my soul to salvage my
reputation, not even for his lordship and ten thousand pounds."

Chapter Ten

The journey from Yorkshire had been interminably long and utterly exhausting, yet Maris felt a surge of excitement as the coach passed through Finchley. She looked greedily at each person walking down the main street, eager for the sight of familiar faces. "Look, Mother, it's Mrs. Pike." But they'd driven past before her mother could rouse herself to wave.

Mr. and Mrs. Cosby, their "couple," were standing on the doorstep, Mrs. Cosby's apron dazzlingly bright in the golden afternoon light. "Oh, ma'am," she called before the door even opened to discharge them. "Oh, ma'am."

Sophie was first down the steps, a Sophie whose radiant health glowed in her cheeks. "Why, Miss Sophie," Mrs. Cosby said, receiving her embrace with startled delight. "Have you grown?"

"Good Yorkshire air, my darling Cosby. I've gained nearly a stone and all my gowns have been let down. Isn't it ridiculous?"

Maris followed her mother. For her, the sojourn in Yorkshire had not been so healthy. In fact, her gown hung on her now. She tied her sashes more tightly and hoped no one would notice. Her mother

had such joy in Sophie's improvement she would
not lessen it for the world.

After greeting the Cosbys, Maris hurried to her
room, seeing everything with new eyes. The pink
hangings of her room seemed far too sweet now, the
pictures of rustic scenes insipid. There were etch-
ings of Grecian ruins in her father's dressing room.
Her mother would not mind if she abstracted them.
She remembered seeing some blue damask, too
heavy for a dress but ideal for drapes.

Maris knew she sketched out these changes to her
room to take her mind off this homecoming. Joyful
though she felt at seeing the familar delights of
home, so much had happened that she felt almost
a stranger. The girl who had left for London in the
spring would never come here again.

After Mrs. Lindel awoke from her nap, Maris assisted her and Mrs. Cosby with unveiling the
furniture and dusting what needed dusting. At first,
Mrs. Cosby asked eager questions about all that they
had seen and done since leaving home. Their an-
swers, however, slow and short, soon gave her the
hint that this might not be the best course to pursue. Mrs. Cosby was an old friend and confidante of
the girls who could not be so badly treated. After
tea, Maris sought her out in the kitchen.

"And what happened then, Miss Maris?" Mrs.
Cosby was so enthralled that she'd put both plump,
rosy elbows on the table, a cardinal sin in her
kitchen.

"I had spent so much time among women by then
that I had all but forgotten that I'd ever had a father. When Mrs. Paladin invoked him, I suddenly
seemed to hear his voice in my head."

"He wouldn't have stood for none of it. Not for

an instant. It was all this Mrs. Paladin's doing, then? A throughly bad woman she must be to have played so wicked a trick."

Once Maris would have agreed with her immediately and would have added examples. Now she was not so certain that the world was painted only in shades of black and white. "Everything she did, so I believe, she did because she loves her daughter. It is not the sort of love my mother has for me."

"So I should say!" Mrs. Cosby put in sharply.

"But it was love that prompted her to act. She couldn't bear the thought of Lilah being a mere farmer's wife when a little effort would see her well established as Lord Danesby's bride."

"Though it would mean a lifetime of misery and regret for them both. You'll pardon me speaking so free, Miss Maris, but that's not my idea of mother love. No. It sounds to me like nothing but pride and covetousness made her act so. She wanted that girl to be rich, not for her sake, oh, no, but for her own. The mother-in-law of our Lord Danesby will be able to swagger it among her high-and-mighty friends and hold her nose very much up, no matter how dirty an arrangement she'd had to make to salve her daughter's honor."

Suddenly, Mrs. Cosby clapped her hand to her mouth and a rich flush deepened the still-girlish pink of her cheeks. "Not that you need worry about your reputation. You're a decent girl and so I'll tell anyone that asks me."

Maris laughed and shook her head. "Don't worry, Cosby darling. No shame attached itself to me. They could not make me marry him for such a foolish reason as my supposedly damaged virtue when it was perfectly plain that it remained entirely unsullied. The footman told them that I'd not been in his lordship's company for even five minutes. There's some sort of rule about that in law, I think. I stopped listening when they started saying the same things over and over again."

"And his lordship?" Mrs. Cosby asked.

"His lordship?"

"What did he say? "

"His lordship was very amiable. He said everything that a gentleman could say under the circumstances and even tried . . ." Despite herself, Maris sighed. "At one point, he even tried to make me believe that he had intended all along to propose to me once I had taken more time to look about me for a husband to my liking."

All in all, it had not been the sort of romantic proposal a girl dreams of, what with four onlookers and a feeling that the gentleman was being forced to say beautiful things. Had they been alone and the words spontaneous, Maris knew she would have consented at once. Then again, perhaps she would not have done so, no matter how her dreams would have prompted her to seize the opportunity with both hands. To have done that, being only concerned with her own longings, would have made her no better than Mrs. Paladin. Maris couldn't be sure, yet it seemed to her that love meant caring as much about the other person's wishes as one's own. She knew perfectly well that she was not made of the stuff a nobleman wants or needs in a wife. Nor, upon reflection, did she possess those qualities that Kenton Danesby wanted and needed.

"They do say he has beautiful manners."

"Who does?"

Mrs. Cosby took a sip of her tea, all but cold now.

"I've not seen him often, you know, though I'm well acquainted with his housekeeper. A fine woman for all she's a trifle slow and Cosby's been known to pass the time of day with his butler, Tremlow. A haughty sort but Cosby says he knows his business."

Maris picked up the thread of her narrative. "Naturally, such a secret could not be kept long."

"I'll wager that Mrs. Paladin creature never buttoned her lip a moment."

"She was rather disgruntled. I'm not sure whether she was more displeased that Lilah had slipped through the net of her weaving or that I had been caught. I think she did believe she could do Mother a good turn by forcing his lordship and me into marriage, having failed to do so well for Lilah."

"What became of the young lady, if I may make so bold?"

"Lilah decided to wait no longer to return to Hay. She will be staying with her aunt. I fear there was a breach between herself and her mother."

"Just as well, by my way of thinking."

"Oh, no," Maris said. "No, that was hardest of all on Mrs. Paladin. She never meant for that to happen, I know. Lilah and I have promised to write. I hope to hear soon that she and Mrs. Paladin have reconciled. It would be a great blessing if they did so before her wedding to Mr. Preston takes place."

"You're too forgiving, Miss Maris."

"Not at all. But to lose her daughter over this foolish ambitiousness would be too cruel. She doesn't deserve that, no one does."

Mrs. Cosby shook her head but said nothing. She stood up and brought the kettle over to freshen the pot as well as bringing another plate of iced biscuits. "But how, Miss Maris, did your uncle come into it?"

"Naturally, I wrote to Mother at once, telling her everything that had happened. She couldn't leave Sophie so she sent my uncle. He took me, bag and baggage, to his home in Yorkshire."

"Miss Sophie's blooming like a rose, Miss Maris. I've not seen her look so since before she took the fever." Maris smiled and lifted her eyebrows in a knowing way. This silence was even more fascinating than the tale of wicked London ways.

"Never say it's a man?"

"Not just a man. A poet."

"A poet?" Mrs. Cosby said incredulously. "She'd be better off with an honest sheep farmer like that there Miss Paladin."

Maris laughed, mentioning old local history, and their talk passed into other areas, new love stories, new and old bones of contention, and all the ordinary ways and means that Maris had missed.

"You didn't mention Miss Menthrip," Maris said when a full account of the Charity Sewing Circle had been given, down to the last stitch in the clothes and the last sultana in the cake.

Mrs. Cosby's round, smiling face lost some of its serenity. "We're all that worried about her, Miss Maris. She's not been ordering half so much food as she used to. The little Gladding girl who used to 'do' for her has been turned off. She gave her a good reference and she's been taken on as the new 'tween maid at Finchley Place but never a word as to why she didn't want her no more. She's not been in church neither and you know she never misses."

"Has Dr. Pike spoken to her?"

"Not yet. But Mrs. Pike tried to see her and she didn't answer the door, though she was at home."

"But this is frightful," Maris said. "I'll tell Mother."

Maris stepped outside when Cosby noticed the fast-setting sun with a shriek of dismay. "Get along with you, do, Miss Maris, or dinner will never be on the table."

The kitchen garden looked neat as Hampton Court's, for Cosby's love of enormous vegetables surpassed even his passion for well-polished silver. Maris breathed a sigh of relief as she passed through the archway in the high brick wall that separated Finchley Old Place's kitchen garden from the formal ones. It wasn't like Mrs. Cosby to let a half-told tale get by her. Fortunately, she'd turned to talking of the village before she could question Maris about her uncle's visit to the metropolis.

A big, bluff man, able to mill down a Luddite with one blow of his hairy fist, he had made the china on the sideboard ring when he'd entered the room, calling for Maris. Mrs. Paladin, interrupted in midgrumble, had dropped her cup, so she greeted Mr. Shelley with tea all down the front breadth of her skirt. This had not improved her temper. Their hired butler had entered behind Mr. Shelley, looking like an ineffectual sheepdog escorting a giant ram, trying to make it all look like his idea.

"Sir, I am Mrs. Paladin," she'd said, trying to gather her dignity.

"I know who you are. Where's m'niece?"

Maris found herself enveloped in an all-encompassing embrace which, after an instant, she returned wholeheartedly, though her arms couldn't possibly meet across his broad back. She felt stitches give in her sleeves. "You must be my Uncle Shelley."

"God's bones, who else would I be?" He held her out at arm's length, searching her face. "You don't remember me, I'm bound, but I remember you

right enough. Four years old, you were, with eyes
the size of a broad crown and dandelion fluff hair
every which way all over your head." He nodded as
if she'd passed inspection. "God's bones but you're
a beauty now."

"You're very kind, Uncle." He must have been six
feet tall and the thick soles and heels on his country man's boots gave him even greater inches. He
wore his white hair so closely cropped that one
could see the pink scalp underneath. His huge
white mustache compensated for any loss on top.
When he smiled, which was often, his cheeks folded
back like concertina pleats, leaving more room for
large white teeth. "Would you care for some breakfast?"

"Breakfast?" He snorted. "I ate mine three hours
ago."

"Then luncheon?"

Mrs. Paladin said, "I fear I am de trop at this
touching family reunion. I will see you later, Mr.
Shelley ."

"Aye, missus. And I'll be seeing you as well."

Maris put forward her theory, a little later, that
Mrs. Paladin had acted unwisely but from the best
motives. "Don't you believe it," her uncle said. "I
know her sort. I read your mother a proper scold
for letting herself be so taken in. I never liked the
scheme of setting up household with some woman
she knew for twenty minutes when she was a girl.
For that's what it comes to, when all's said and
done."

"People change, I suppose, and not always for the
better."

"Don't you believe it," he said again. "The person

you are at seventeen is who'll you'll be your whole life."

"Heavens, I hope not!" Maris cried, thinking of her own sins of identity and ability.

"That Paladin woman proves my point. I pried it out of your mother that this Paladin woman was a liar and a cheat even then, willing to do down her best friend for a chance at a beau. I've told your mother what a proper dry-boots I thought her to be such a fool."

Maris drew herself up. "Mother is no fool, sir. She was forced to make shift as best she could."

"Meaning I ought to have paid down my blunt for your come-out?"

"I have not said so. But I will not have my mother sneered at for her sacrifices when those sacrifices were for me."

"I'm not one to hide my teeth, girl." Uncle Shelley puffed through his mustache, setting it fluttering.

"In truth, Uncle? I should not have guessed it."

He laughed, his broad shoulders shaking, the china tinkling anew. "That's the way. Hit out. I've no time for a milk-and-water miss and neither has any other man worth his salt."

"How is Mother? And Sophie?"

"I've letters for you from both of them in my cloak bag. But you'll see 'em yourself end of the week."

"Then Sophie is well enough to travel?" Maris cried out happily.

"She's much improved but you mistook my meaning. You're going to them."

"I beg your pardon?" Maris said, drawing back.

"How soon can you pack your fribbles? We'll go

north as soon as damnit. I've one or two errands to
tend to first then we'll away on the post road."

"But I can't . . ." Maris scolded herself. Could it be
that she cherished even now the faintest, tiniest
hope of seeing Lord Danesby again? His only feeling toward her now must be one of disgust if not
absolute detestation. Though they had parted well
at Durham House, he going so far as to kiss her
hand, he would never permit himself to associate
with one who had shared with him that ultimate embarrassment.

Mr. Shelley took no notice of her hesitation.
"Your aunt is agog to see you. The entertainments
she's planning may not have that London air but I
doubt you'll mind. You look a sensible sort, niece."

"Thank you, Uncle." Even in the midst of her interior confusion, she would have been much too
hard to please had she found her bluff, bold uncle
anything but charming. He seemed to live to lift
burdens off confused young women's shoulders.

What he said to Mrs. Paladin was never divulged
but the constant stream of complaints dried up. He
paid for Lilah to return to Hay, broke the lease of
the house, and arranged for the paying off of the
servants. He even offered Mrs. Paladin the return of
her half of the rent. Mrs. Paladin declined haugh-
tily enough at first, though later changed her mind
when she discovered that Tunbridge Wells Spa was
more expensive than she'd been told.

Only when he proposed calling upon Lord
Danesby did Maris try to stop the whirlwind that was
her Yorkshire uncle. "Why do you want to do that?"

He looked over his magnifying lenses at her,
pushing aside the sheets of the lease. "I want to see

him for myself. You've said little enough about him."

"He is a gentleman, Uncle, and did all that a gentleman could have done under the circumstances. It was I who refused to marry, not him."

"I know it," he said. "To my way of thinking you couldn't have done anything else. And I don't care a jot or a tittle what all those grand folks were telling you what must be done. God's bones! Their daughters' honors might be so easily lost but I've known your mother since she was in her cradle and no child of hers would ever do wrong."

"I hope you told her so."

"I did."

"Then you needn't see his lordship," Maris said a few minutes later, after her uncle had returned to his reading.

"Eh? No, no. Certainly not. My God, couldn't she find a lawyer to vet this paper before she signed it?"

Yet the next day, when she couldn't find him, the butler told her where he'd gone. She'd spent a good deal of time asking herself why that meeting haunted her imagination. Had Lord Danesby been cold or welcoming? What measure had he taken of Mr. Shelley? Did he understand that his hearty manner was not that of a Captain Sharp trying to bluff his way into his lordship's good graces but of an honest man who dealt with the world as he himself would like to be treated? Mr. Shelley had no time for pretty phrases or delicate fencing. He was a blunderbuss and cutlass man.

Yet, when she saw her uncle again, she asked no questions. If Lord Danesby had refused to see him or had been coldly polite, she did not wish to know it. If he'd been the merry friend she'd met and liked, that, in its own way, would have been worse. She didn't want him to suffer because she'd refused him and yet it didn't seem right somehow that he should be unchanged.

The next day, after breakfast, Mrs. Lindel wrapped up a basket of Mrs. Cosby's iced biscuits, a bottle of her own black currant wine, and a copy of the latest scandalous novel, acquired in town. "One or the other of these should get you through Miss Menthrip's defenses," she said confidently.

"Don't you want to go, Mother?"

"Not this time. You have a better chance of getting over the threshold than I. You look too young to be our spy."

"I'll go," Sophie volunteered. "I like Miss Menthrip. She says what she thinks."

"No, indeed. I am going to finish marking your hems if I die for it." She squinted at her youngest daughter. "Maris," Mrs. Lindel demanded, "has your sister grown *again*?"

"Indeed, yes. I noticed it this morning. There's nothing for it, Mother, but to bind heavy books to her head." Sophie shied the one in her hand at her sister, who skipped out the door with a merry, "Missed me!"

Maris paused for an instant, out of sight, then nodded with satisfaction when she heard Sophie say, "She seems happier now we are home, Mother."

"I hope so, dearest. I hate to see my girls moping about."

"You needn't worry about me, at any rate. I'm perfectly happy."

"Even though Mr. Delmore remained in York-shire?"

"Even though Mr. Delmore remained in York-shire. I am too young to be thinking of poets. Besides, he promised to write to me and I think he will. Poets will take any excuse to put pen to paper."

Along the road to the village, the trees were still green but with a sere tinge to their leaves that spoke of autumn's near arrival. The hay had been gathered and stood in tall shooks, while crows creaked and called in the large dead tree by the crossroads. But the sun shone down with a friendly heat from the deep azure sky and smaller birds still hopped and flitted about the puddles in the main street.

Miss Menthrip's white door with the iron hinges stayed resolutely shut despite Maris's knocking. A casement window stood open a crack, a fold of the white curtain hanging within having kept the latch from closing. Maris worked a gloved finger under the opening, tugging until it swung reluctantly outward.

"Miss Menthrip? It's I, Maris Lindel. I want to talk to you."

She heard a gusty sigh and the thump of her walking stick as Miss Menthrip crossed the floor. A few moments later, there came the snap of the lock springing open. Miss Menthrip, her dress dusty black, her hair as tightly controlled as ever, waved her in. "I know you," she said, her voice harsh. "You'll keep it up until I give in so I might as well give in now."

"Everyone's very concerned about you, Miss Menthrip. You haven't been to church in so long," Maris said as she followed her into the kitchen at the back of the cottage.

"Of course, I haven't been to church. How can I go when I can't afford to put even a shilling in the bag? A shilling? Ha, I can't manage a groat."

Maris lifted the basket to the well-scrubbed table. "Why can't you?"

Miss Menthrip laughed. "Matter of fact child, aren't you? I can't because I've no money barring the few pounds I've kept in the stocking's foot. Every other farthing has been lost." Though her voice rang with something akin to triumph, her posture slumped as she fell onto a chair.

"Yet . . ." Maris paused before passing on the gossip. "I'd always heard that your brother left you well beforehand with the world."

"Talk about me, do they? Well, they'll have plenty more to say now. Soon they'll start to pity me. But I'll not take charity from anyone. What's in the basket?"

"Not charity, I promise." Miss Menthrip's eyes widened in their nests of wrinkles when she saw the book.

"I've had to let my membership in the lending library cease which was the most unkindest cut of all."

"I met the man who wrote it," Maris said. "Everyone calls him Pinkie but he's really a French marquis. Or at least, his father was but he has some hopes of reclaiming his title from King Louis."

"You've met a deal of grand people, I'll warrant." Miss Menthrip would not sink so low as to ask questions, but she was obviously agog to hear all the details.

Maris told her enough to content her for the moment, and to make the *roman à clef* more intelligible. Then, tactfuly pouring out a glass of wine, she returned to the purpose of her visit. "How did you come to such straits, dear Miss Menthrip?"

"It was that solicitor-johnny my brother made trustee. I told him that Jackie Household had a nasty, cheating, furtive eye but nothing would do for Worrel but that he give this business to his old friend's boy. 'His father was the best of men,' he said to me. 'I know this boy is just such another. He even looks like Jack.' I tell you plain, if he looked like Jack Household, it wasn't his mother's fault!"

Maris did not look shocked, only pouring out a little more wine to calm Miss Menthrip's cough, sparked by this bit of old scandal. "This Mr. Household has lost your money on the 'Change?" she asked.

"Worse than that. It seemed he made quite a tidy fortune by some hasty dealing just before Waterloo. My little nest egg had grown to the size of a roc's egg. I'd even begun to plan what I'd do with it, counting my blessings too soon, as it turned out."

"What happened?"

"Master Jackie absconded to the Continent, taking with him not only the profits of his venture but all my capital as well."

This was worse than Maris had imagined. She waited until Miss Menthrip stopped coughing again, disquieted by the hacking rattle at the end of the paroxysm. She wished very much that her mother were here to judge the severity of that cough.

"Surely he is being pursued?"

"Oh, yes. I'm not the only one in this basket, thank heaven. Others, who did not entrust every cent to Master Jackie, have hired Runners to go after him. But he was three days gone before anyone realized what he'd done so the trail is very cold. There are so many English going to Europe these days, there is but little hope they can find one shifty-eyed brute among so many."

"I'm sure they'll catch him."

"Maybe they will and maybe they won't. If they do, who's to say but that he will have spent it all before they hunt him down. It's not Jackie Household's future that has me in a proper swivet. It's my own." The wrinkled hands folded on the knob of the stick tightened until the white knuckles showed but could not slow their frightened trembling.

"I shall have to go into the almshouse," she said, her voice quavering, sounding like an elderly lady plagued by confusion instead of the forthright spinster. "I visited there once and I've never forgotten it. Outside the gate it said, WOODRUFF HOUSE FOR INDIGENT SPINSTERS AND WIDOWS. ESTABLISHED 1744. They all wore snuff-colored bonnets and cloaks with a large white cross on the back. You never heard anyone speak. And they were never allowed to be alone—they even slept all together in a long dormitory, bed after bed."

"That won't happen," Maris said, stooping to slip an arm about Miss Menthrip's shoulders. She was shocked by how thin and fragile her friend seemed. Miss Menthrip must be trying to support existence on the cheapest, plainest food, and not much of it either.

"You're a good child, Maris Lindel. But I tell you plain. I'd rather die than go to such a place."

"I promise you; it will not come to that."

Chapter Eleven

Lucy's eyes filled with tears as she embraced her friend as the chime of the noon bell mingled with the hysterical yapping of Gog and Magog. "You look so different," she said.

"Do I? You ought to see Sophie."

"I can't quite tell what it is. An air of fashion, perhaps. Be quiet, Gog! Get down, Magog."

"I doubt it. But look at you. Why in heaven's name are you wearing that cap?"

Mrs. Pike, waiting her turn to greet the prodigal, laughed ironically, silencing the dogs. "Well you may ask, Maris. I have been waiting for your return so that you might talk some sense into this daughter of mine. I tell her it is ridiculous for her to throw away her youth even for a brother."

Maris shook hands with the vicar's wife. "Which brother?"

"Ryan, of course. He's been asked to teach at a rather prestigious school and nothing will do but that his sister should come to keep house for him."

"Ryan is to teach?" Maris marveled. "But he's just a boy himself."

"It's a great honor, Dr. Pike tells me, to be so singled out at his age. Dr. Valega at Oxford recommended him for the post, saying that he himself had no more to teach him so he might as well teach others. Though why, in the name of goodness, he has to drag Lucy along, I shall never understand."

"It's only for a year, Mama," Lucy said wearily. Maris had heard that tone in her own voice more than once this summer and knew it meant Lucy had been arguing in the same words until she was exhausted.

"If you can be spared from the household," Maris said, changing the subject, "Mother asks if you and Lucy will be our guests at dinner tonight."

Mrs. Pike's eyes softened as she smiled. "I meant to invite the three of you, but I suppose those rascals of mine may fend for themselves for once. I shall inform Mr. Pike. I do not think he will object."

"Tell him, if you wish, that we are to discuss what is to be done to aid Miss Menthrip."

"Never say you have been to see her? Maris Lindel, you are a worker of wonders."

"Not I, ma'am. I was merely the scouting party in advance of the main body. My mother is with Miss Menthrip now. She believes that the first order of business must be to have the doctor call upon her. I wonder if you would be good enough to ask him to do so at his earliest opportunity."

"I'll do so at once. Tell me, though. Is she very ill?"

"Mother thinks not, but does not like the cough that hangs upon her. There have been some reverses in her personal economy and she has been skimping on food."

"Oh, these old women are all the same," Mrs. Pike said, peering in the hall mirror to be certain her own cap was straight. "They will believe that they must conserve every farthing and end up spending themselves. I wonder if she would care for that pig's cheek? I was saving it for a cold collation on Sunday, but . . ." She walked purposefully toward the back of the house, still talking to herself.

Lucy seized Maris's hand and ran with her up the stairs to her room. "Hurry, before she thinks of a task for me."

"Are you really going off with Ryan to a school?"

"Yes, I am. He'll never manage without someone to care for him. There are some married house-masters so I shall not be quite without feminine companionship and the masters' chambers are charming. Sixteenth century buildings, you know."

"Surely he can hire someone to care for him."

"No one can do it like I can. You know how absentminded he can be when he's studying. If I'm not there to feed him and remind him about his classes, he won't stay long at the school. And this is such an important step for him. There are excellent Roman remains at Chitterton and Ryan hopes there may be a villa at Medley. He said that the landscape is precisely what the Romans liked. The governors of the school have given him permission to excavate when he's not teaching."

Lucy wore her most obstinate look, exactly like a pretty white mule. Her mother must have known it was pointless to argue with Lucy when she looked like that. "What does your father say?"

"Oh, he quotes something about laboring seven years for Rachel, which doesn't seem to apply, does it?"

"Not very well. Is Ryan pleased?"

"Yes. When he asked me, he made it clear that he thought it a very good opportunity for me as well. There are bound to be unmarried masters and as the only single female at Medley, I should have a success even were I more ill-favored than I am."

Maris leaned back on her elbows on her friend's white coverlet, squinting at her. "I've learned a great deal in London, one way or another," she said. "You're not really plain at all, Lucy."

"Oh, come. With this thin hair and crooked nose?"

"Hmmm. Take off that cap."

"No. I'm resigned to my fate."

"Never resign yourself to fate, Lucy. If I'd done that, I'd be Lady Danesby."

"What?" Lucy leapt off the stool, where she'd been drooping like a wilted lily. "Tell me everything at once!"

"I shall tell you everything if you let me fix your hair. I shall anyway, so you might as well listen while I work."

She was so enthralled by the tale Maris told that she paid no attention to what Maris was doing until the sewing scissors came out. "No, what are you doing?"

"This." And Maris cut.

Though Lucy shuddered at each snip of the scissors and invoked the name of her mother like a sacrifice calling upon a goddess, Maris was ruthless.

With her soft hair taken out of a scraped-back topknot, a few pieces cut short and forced to curl about her forehead, her eyes looked softer, larger, and more vulnerable. The wispy curls also concealed the few spots on her forehead. A low chignon, nestled against her neck, changed the shape of her face and hid her ears.

"Let me see your dresses," Maris demanded.

Lucy was leaning toward the small mirror, all her

vicar father had allowed her, moving her head so
that she could see herself. She waved toward the
wardrobe and didn't turn her attention away from
her face until she heard the first rip.

"Maris!"

Maris flourished a scrap of lace tucker aloft like a
savage exulting over his first scalp. "So perish all
such pathetic scraps. Only spinsters and invalids
wear these little lace borders anymore. For the rest,
décolletage is lower than ever."

"But what will Mama say?"

"Nothing, when she sees that I am wearing the
same thing. Now, come help me rip all these off."

"No, no. Maris, you're going too far," she gasped
when Maris picked up another gown and began to
struggle with the lace.

"Very well. Put on this one. If you don't like it, I
shall sew it on again myself."

But when Lucy saw her figure displayed for the
first time, Maris using her own sash to remodel the
fit of the too-large dress (one of Mrs. Pike's cut
down), she turned and twisted, growing more excited by the minute. "There's a pier glass in the best
spare room," she said. "I want to see all of me."

One glance was enough. She turned to Maris
with tears in her eyes. For an instant, Maris felt a
burning sense of guilt. Then Lucy smiled. "You're
my fairy godmother," she said.

"There's nothing much I can do except spend my
life in good works," Maris answered.

"Can you never go back to London?"

Maris shook her head. "No. Not until the stories
stop flying and they would only begin anew if I return. Perhaps I could go back if I found a husband

of greater note than Lord Danesby, but what are the odds of that?"

"I still don't understand why you didn't agree. I would have, in an instant."

"I don't think you would have. To have a husband that you adored but who despised you? I wouldn't wish anyone to suffer that torture. Besides, that is no fit fate for either of us. We are young, we are blonde, we have nothing to be afraid of."

"Except Mama," Lucy said. She turned again to the mirror. "Do you think she'll be angry?"

"No. But she might not let you go to Medley until after the winter assemblies. I think the sight of you like this might reanimate her ambitions of a good marriage."

"They've certainly awakened mine. I look . . . I look . . ."

"Say it," Maris urged.

"I look so pretty." Then the tears came.

Maris still had a damp patch on her shoulder when she led Lucy downstairs to meet Mrs. Pike to escort her to Finchley Old Place, both their cloaks over her arm. Mrs. Pike turned, her usual affectionate scoldings drying on her lips. "Good God in heaven!" she exclaimed, the first time she'd taken the name of the Lord in vain in her own house.

"You asked me to persuade her out of her cap, ma'am," Maris said.

"What next, Maris? Water into wine?" She held out her arms to her daughter and Lucy flew down the last few stairs.

"You're not angry, Mama?"

"Angry?" She cupped Lucy's face in her hands, gazing at her with wonderment. "I confess I should have said no if you had asked me for permission. I would have been wrong. But what have you done to your dinner dress?"

"Maris said no one is wearing tuckers anymore except for old maids and invalids."

"Quick, put on your cloak before your father sees. I don't object but he surely will."

It was too late, however. The vicar came down the hallway to bid his wife and daughter a pleasant evening. He did not appear to notice that Lucy's figure was considerably more on display than was usual. He did abjure her to wrap up well and held his wife back a moment when she would have followed the girls at once out the door.

"What did he say?" Lucy asked tremulously when Mrs. Pike joined them in the garden.

"One believes one knows a man after more than twenty years of marriage." She seemed dazed.

"But what did he say, Mama?"

"He reminded me that the daughters of Israel adorned themselves to dance before David and reminded me that his mother's jewelry was still in the bank. A very fine set of garnets and some quite good pearls, Lucy. They will become you very well."

Dealing with the question of Miss Menthrip, however, took more ingenuity than a few clips with a scissors and some determined yanking of stitches. The chief problem was money. Neither the Pikes, with their many sons, nor the Lindels, after their recent expenses, had any to spare. "I can pay the doctor's bill," Mrs. Lindel said. "But I don't know where to lay my hands on enough for this trip to Bath."

"Must it be Bath?" Mrs. Pike asked. "Surely there are lesser spas."

"No, he said that the water at Bath is the most ef-

ficacious in the matter of weakened lungs. We
should also have to find someone to accompany her
hence. In her present state, she cannot be expected
to find lodgings or fend for herself."

"I'll go," Lucy said, only a breath faster than Maris.

"Yes?" Mrs. Pike answered. "And what of your
brother?"

"There's no point in discussing it until we find
the money," Mrs. Lindel reminded them. "Is there
anything in the parish funds? Might not some charity money be diverted to this cause?"

Mrs. Pike shook her head regretfully. "There've
been many calls on the parish these last few months.
Mr. Pike says that at most we may offer a widow's
mite but no more until next year."

Sophie had been listening intently. "It won't do any
good to send Miss Menthrip to Bath if she must still
live in her cottage when she returns. Not two windows
fit tightly in their frames and the door rattles with
every breeze. She'll only fall sick again if these matters are not mended. I know she meant to have them
seen to this year but now someone else must do it."

"I hate to say this," Mrs. Lindel said, "but perhaps
the almshouse is the best place for her."

"Couldn't she live with us?" Sophie asked. "I'm
very fond of Miss Menthrip."

Maris caught the glance that passed between the
two mothers. Neither of them could afford to add
another person to their households, and even if
that were not the case, adding an elderly woman
famous for her sharp tongue and freely offered
opinions would not be a gain to harmony. The best
answer would be to keep her in her own house,
snug and independent, but that solution still required money.

Did she know anyone with money to spare? She was not on terms with any of the grand people she had met in London to solicit their assistance. The wealthy nobles of England already received countless charitable requests; the plight of one old woman would not stir their hearts. The great charitable institutions did not hand out funds, preferring to absorb the deserving poor into their rigid embraces.

"I will ask Mr. Pike to poll the parish committee when it meets next week. Perhaps some of them will be able to determine a course for Miss Menthrip's relief."

"Miss Menthrip doesn't wish for charity," Maris said.

Mrs. Pike scoffed. "Such pride is foolish when a case is desperate. If she is destitute, she must take charity and be properly thankful."

"True," Mrs. Lindel said. "I'm afraid her pride must go to the wall in this instance. I sympathize with her very much; I should feel much the same. Yet one must face facts."

Maris knew, in her heart, that the two mothers spoke truthfully. Yet she could so easily imagine herself an elderly spinster without a relation in the world in such straits as those of Miss Menthrip. She could only hope that she could summon the same proud spirit Miss Menthrip showed. How much better to keep one's pride, even if, strictly speaking, one could not afford to.

"Does Miss Menthrip own her cottage outright?" Maris asked.

"She holds the freehold, Maris, but the ground is only on a ninety-nine-year lease."

"Who owns that, then?"

"Why, his lordship, of course."

"Of course." She remembered hearing about that arrangement, so strange, so English, when she was a little girl. She'd spent quite some time trying to puzzle out how one could own a house but not the land. What if you wanted to move? What if there was an earthquake and your house fell into the ground?

Perhaps it was this mention of Lord Danesby that put a plot into Maris's head. But the mixture of the parish committe, Lord Danesby's ownership of the land, and their need for money turned and tumbled in her brain. Lord Danesby had money. Lord Danesby sat on the parish committee.

But how could she introduce his name into this conclave? To mention him, even in passing, would distress her mother. If Mrs. Pike did not already know the tale of Maris and his lordship, either Mrs. Lindel or Lucy would soon inform her of it. Maris knew she must take great care to look unconscious of any connection between them when Mrs. Pike questioned her about him.

In the end, though, it was Sophie who brought him up. "I don't know why you don't just ask Lord Danesby for the money. He must be rich enough to send dozens of ladies, old and young, to Bath or anywhere else for that matter. He's in residence now; Mr. Cosby told me so. Why don't you ask Lord Danesby?"

"No," Mrs. Lindel said.

"Out of the question," Mrs. Pike said.

"Goodness, no. How could we?" Lucy asked.

"Why not?" Maris said, echoing her sister, who, she vowed, would receive an especially lavish present from her older sister this year. She did not want to see Lord Danesby herself. The part of her life when she would hide behind tree trunks and peer around corners to catch a glimpse of him had ended. Yet, as he had the resources to send Miss Menthrip on a trip that might save her life, it seemed sensible to ask him for it.

"He's a single gentleman," Mrs. Pike said. "It would be most indelicate to approach him with such a suggestion. If he had a wife, of course, it would prove a different matter. But bachelor gentlemen are not interested in charity cases."

"It's not a charity case," Sophie persisted. "It's Miss Menthrip. He has a fortune; why shouldn't he use some of it to help Miss Menthrip? You could ask him, Mrs. Pike."

Mrs. Pike refused, holding up her hands. "Impossible. We are not on calling terms with Lord Danesby. How could we be with no lady of the house upon whom we might leave cards?"

Sophie turned to her mother. "You could call on him, Mother."

"Such things are better left to the vicar. Perhaps Mr. Pike could call upon his lordship tomorrow?"

"Impossible. Mr. Pike is away to visit his old friend Mr. Ratliff, recently given a living in Bruxton parish. They are going to visit the bishop and shall not return for several days at least. I am not even certain he will be available to attend the parish committee this month."

Maris did not know how much her mother had told Sophie of why they had not returned to London or why their visit to Yorkshire was so prolonged. Yet she didn't suppose it would have mattered very much to Sophie if she had known of the incident at Durham House. She had a very straightforward brain. If one needed money, one went to people who had it. She didn't want sympathy and half-hearted assistance but action. Maris entirely agreed

with her yet boggled at the idea of seeing Lord
Danesby again. She'd rather hoped she'd never be
forced to speak to him, however often she might
glimpse him in the distance.

As the Pikes took their leave, with much discussed
but little settled, Maris drew Lucy aside. "Be ready
to walk with me at half past ten tomorrow. I have a
matter of great importance and need your help."

"Certainly," Lucy said, agog. "What it is?"

"Tomorrow. Don't fail me. Wear the blue dress."

By embroidering ceaselessly upon every detail of
her London experiences, Maris managed to keep
Lucy from wondering where they were headed for
quite some time. Eventually, however, her attention
was distracted from a description of Durham House's
grandeur. "Surely this is the drive to Finchley Place?"
she exclaimed. "Maris, where are we going?"

"To see his lordship, of course."

"To see . . . ? Oh, no, no, no!"

"Come now, Lucy, don't fail me. I must see him
about Miss Menthrip and I must not go alone."

"You tricked me. Oh, Maris, how could you? I
can't go. What would my mother say?"

"She'd say you did right in not letting me go
alone. I don't know why you are making such a fuss.
He's just a man like any other. A bit better-looking
perhaps but nothing to be frightened of."

"How can you say that? This is Lord Danesby you
are speaking of. Lord Danesby." If Maris had not
taken a firm hold of Lucy's wrist, she would have
darted away home, heedless of her dress and dignity
alike.

"What of it? He can't eat you. You needn't even

speak to him beyond a civil how do you do. But I must not go to Finchley Place alone, not after what passed at Durham House. I'm very sorry indeed that I tricked you into accompanying me but you must see that I need you, Lucy." Privately, Maris thought she'd been quite right in not telling Lucy where they were going immediately. They never would have come even this far if she had.

As it was, it took nearly as long to walk the drive up to the house as it had taken to reach the drive itself. Lucy's knees were apt to give out and Maris could feel her friend's trembling through their linked arms. If Maris had been delivering Lucy to a dragon's den to meet the usual fate of virgins, she could not have been more terrified. Maris tried to be kind, remembering that Lucy had not spent any time at all in Lord Danesby's company. She still thought of him as an unattainable ideal, uncorrupted by contact with ordinary mortals.

Maris was happy to discover that while she could remember feeling just that way, no trace of hero worship remained, search her soul as she might. Kenton Danesby was a man, nothing more.

His house stood on a sward of perfectly shaved grass, as though it had grown there. Of red brick touched with pale Caen stone, it wore its stone traceries and large, glittering windows with the confidence of a woman who knows her jewelry is not only genuine but beyond price. Parallel staircases flowed down from the front terrace as though eagerly inviting guests to enter.

For a moment, Maris felt a pang of loss. This house, smiling at her in the golden sunshine, could have been hers. She could have known every corner with the love such beauty demanded as its due.

Then she smiled at herself, realizing it was fortu-
itous that she'd not seen Finchley Place before his
lordship had proposed. She might have been able
to resist him out of altruism but not his house.

Then a baying of hounds shattered the peace and
quiet of the countryside. Lucy gave one shriek before she turned and fled, skirt hiked high, bonnet
tumbling down her back, for the shelter of the trees
beyond the lawn.

Maris stood her ground, though it sounded as
though the Devil's own pack headed toward her.
They came around the corner of the house, a brown
and white flood, every liver-colored nose lifted, every
whip tail a-wag. At once, they raced loping over the
emerald grass to surround her in a panting, sniffing,
never-still pack. She patted and petted every one she
could reach—there were no more than ten, if so
many—saying, "Yes, sir. Good boy. Down, sir. Indeed
you may sniff my gloves. Good boy."

Then one, impatient for his meed of attention,
nudged her hard behind the knees and she stum-
bled, falling to the ground. One hound yelped as
she put her hand down on his paw. The rest, in-
trigued by this new stage in their acquaintance,
pushed closer to see what she'd do next. Maris
laughed when one hound, not content with sniffing
her hands, licked her face, pushing his long nose
under her bonnet to do so.

Kenton, coming around the house in pursuit of
his dogs, saw a lady in distress and advanced at a run
to school the animals. Then he heard her laugh,
ringing out, carrying with it all the joy and happiness in the world, and he paused, unsure if he was
asleep or awake. How often had he awakened in the
night over the past months, hearing that laughter

fading along the corridors of his mind? He called himself a fool when he returned to himself, for why should the thought of losing Miss Lindel's laughter cause him any distress? Yet always in those first moments after waking, he knew despair at his loss.

"Get by, sir," Maris said. "Let me up, you foolish creatures." She looked past the milling dogs and saw him. Suddenly, she smiled, sharing her amusement at the farce of her position. "I meant to be very dignified, Lord Danesby. As you see, I have failed."

He reached out both hands over the dogs' backs, helping her to her feet. For a moment, she stood with her hands clasped in both of his. He searched her face. Barring a muddy smear from an inquisitive nose, she looked just as she had in London. No, not quite. Her gaze met his without a trace of self-consciousness. No shyness made her look away while a blush burned itself out in her cheeks. Nor did her hands quiver in his. His sense of loss, of having just failed to catch a precious stone tossed to him, engulfed him once again. Maris Lindel was no longer in love with him.

She took her hands from his grasp on the pretext of shaking out her twisted skirts. "You look well," she said. "Have you had a pleasant summer?"

"Very pleasant, Miss Lindel. The racing was excellent."

"And now you prepare to hunt?"

He looked down at the dogs and laughed. "With this motley crew? I fear not. I don't actually enjoy hunting anymore, not since I took a bad spill in Quorn country. I wasn't hurt very badly—barring a broken arm—but I had to shoot my horse. It happened to be one I was especially fond of."

What in heaven's name possessed him to go babbling out that morbid story? He had, in spare moments, envisioned their next meeting. Kenton had promised himself that he would be suave, putting her at her ease, and charming her without apparent effort. He wanted, he supposed, to instill in her the same sense of loss he felt, to know what she had refused. Seeing her now, he realized how childish that ambition was. He didn't want her to suffer even an instant of what he felt now, the knowledge that he'd been an utter fool and showed no signs of improving.

"I can understand how that might put you off hunting," Maris said. She looked over her shoulder. "Might I trouble you to return your dogs to their pen, my lord? My friend, Miss Pike, is easily alarmed and dogs frighten her. All except Gog and Magog, her father's pugs."

"Certainly." He put two fingers to his lips, whistling sharply. Did a slight gleam of admiration appear in Maris's eyes? "My kennel man will come collect them."

Hudnall and Dominic appeared, deep in conversation. Kenton felt a pang of jealousy when Maris seemed to appreciate the sight of Dom's tall form. He supposed Dom was a rather good-looking chap, if you took away that air he had of not being quite present. He introduced them somewhat ungraciously but neither seemed to notice.

"It's a delight to meet you at last, Miss Lindel," Dom said, bowing over her hand.

"There seems to be a young lady in the trees over there, Dom," Kenton said. "Would you be a good fellow and reassure her that the dogs will soon be kenneled?"

"I'll even undertake to bring her down from the tree. What is her name?"

"Lucy Pike," Maris said. "She's rather nervous of dogs and of Lord . . . and of strangers."

"I'm entirely harmless, I assure you."

Kenton and Maris watched Dom lope off in the direction of the trees. "Never tell me that Miss Pike is afraid of me?"

"Yes, my lord. You are rather an intimidating person to a young miss fresh from the country." Her smile was slightly ironical, a new expression which charmed him as much as her wide-eyed simplicity did.

"You were never intimidated by me, Miss Lindel, or indeed by anything."

"You are wrong, my lord. But you called me Maris once upon a time." Was she flirting with him? He decided she was but, lowering thought, only as she might have flirted with a fossilized friend of the family.

"A gentleman is allowed to use a lady's Christian name when proposing to her. He reverts to her surname when he is refused."

"Then you must certainly continue to call me Miss Lindel." Without the slightest acknowledgment of his reference to their past, she gave a last shake to her skirts and straightened her bonnet from its drunken pose over her left ear. "There. Now that I am respectable again, shall I tell you why I have called?"

"You're not respectable just yet." He reached out to rub away the mud from her cheek only to have her flinch away before he could touch her. For the first time, her eyes shifted away from his gaze.

"Will you come into the house for some tea, Miss Lindel?"

"You are very kind, my lord. I shall wait for my friend, if I may?"

"This house is yours," he said, reverting to the grand phrase of Spanish hosts. He'd said it before, to other guests, but he'd never meant it quite so earnestly. Whatever she wanted, and he felt sure she wanted something or she never would have come, she could have.

"So that's your Miss Lindel, is it?" Dom said as they waved to the back of the landau taking the young ladies home.

"Yes."

"How soon do you leave for Bath?"

"Tomorrow. Do you care to accompany me?"

"In the same spirit that Miss Lindel accompanies her elderly friend? To assist you and see you come to no mischief?"

"The mischief's done," Kenton said. "If I hadn't been such a fool in town . . . well, it's all spilt milk now. But I hope to show her a better side of me in Bath than she saw in London. I think she liked my roses at any rate."

"So she'll be your betrothed by—what—Tuesday next? Three days for a special license and then 'ring out wild bells.'"

Kenton sighed deeply. "In a romance, perhaps. But there's a harder task ahead of me than slaying a dragon or redeeming the Holy Grail. I have to make her fall in love with me again."

Chapter Twelve

To Maris's surprise, her mother had not scolded her for approaching his lordship with the problem of what to do with Miss Menthrip. On the contrary, she praised her. "That was very well thought of, Maris. You showed great courage."

"He's not an ogre," she said, finding it odd that she should find it necessary to defend Lord Danesby to her mother in the same words she had used to Lucy. "I knew he would find it in his heart to be generous."

"I did not mean that he would be cruel or indifferent to Miss Menthrip's plight, though I would not have thought to approach him in the matter. If there were a lady at the manor, perhaps I should have done so."

"Is it only women who care what becomes of those less fortunate? I am certain there are many fine philanthropists who are men."

Mrs. Lindel merely smiled at her daughter's heat. "I imagine there are many such, though I have had not heard that his lordship is among their number. Yet you must admit it took some courage on your part to speak to his lordship at all, after your last meeting."

"Mother," Maris began, feeling the time was ripe, "what did Uncle Shelley say to him?"

"Uncle Shelley?"

"When he was in London, I know he called upon his lordship."

"Did he? I'm afraid we never discussed it. My brother assured me that he felt the matter was closed and no good purpose could come of pursuing it further. He thought it very well done of you to refuse his lordship's kindly meant offer. I agree with him. It would have made you look guilty."

"How do you know I'm not?"

Mrs. Lindel laughed. "Don't be so foolish, Maris. Even if I were blind and irretrievably stupid, you're not the sort of fool who throws her cap over the windmill and counts the world well lost for love. Lord Danesby may be your beau ideal but you are, I hope, a properly raised girl."

"My . . . my beau ideal?"

"You have been in love with him, or rather the idea of him, since you were fifteen, have you not? You and Lucy Pike both."

Maris stared in disbelief at her mother. Was this the sweet, rather vague woman she'd lived with for so long? Mrs. Lindel laughed again, this time at her dumbfounded daughter's expression. "Don't tell me you didn't think I knew? When every scrap of paper in your room had some variation of 'Lady Danesby' scrawled over and over upon it? When I found drawings of your supposed monogram on the edge of every picture you sketched? I may not be clever, my dear, but I'm observant."

Maris chuckled at herself and then laughed with her mother. "Did you ever see the description of our wedding I wrote for the *Gazette?* Twelve white horses drew the carriage, if you please, while no one less exalted than the Archbishop of Canterbury performed the ceremony. I believe the King was in attendance, miraculously restored to full health."

"Did doves hold up your veil?" Mrs. Lindel inquired. "When I was going to marry the doctor's son, doves were to hold up the edges of my veil and two marchionesses were to carry my train. *I* was to be married in Westminster."

"The doctor's son? I never heard this tale."

"It was so long ago. I hardly remember his name now but he was the most beautiful young man, at least to my nine-year-old eyes. I remember he had very straight brows which made him look deliciously stern. I was certain he'd committed some terrible crime. I vowed that when he was arrested, I would pine beneath his prison window, dying in the same hour that they hung him."

"Before or after you were married in Westminster?" Maris asked wonderingly, fascinated by the light this confession threw on her own imaginings.

"No, that was the version where he was reprieved and his wicked uncle—who had kidnapped the rightful heir and left him to die in a field where he was rescued by Dr. Dowdy—that was his name! Gregory Dowdy." She smiled distantly, as if looking across the years at the whimsical child she'd been.

"What about the wicked uncle?" Maris demanded.

"Oh, what nonsense I thought of. Naturally, Gregory was no mere doctor's son. After I saved him from the prison or the terrible fate that awaited him, he'd discover he was the rightful heir to a dukedom and return to me in gratitude. Then we'd have the grand ceremony. I remember, yes, I remember I was determined to have a five-guinea lace veil. To me, the height of opulence."

Maris came and put her arms about her mother's waist. "I wish I'd told you sooner."

"But where would be the relish in that? These dreams wither if they are spoken while we believe them. Every girl finds some unattainable man to adore. It is a safe way to play with those feelings that make up a woman's life. When we are ready for real love, we remember our play and it adds a gloss to the sometimes dreary round of a marriage." Once again, she seemed to be looking at things in the past, things Maris could neither share nor see. Yet she could glimpse, dimly, that these matters lay in her future.

"Must it be dreary?"

"What, my dear? No, but it cannot always be like our dreams. Dreams end with 'and they lived happily ever after.' The rest of us must go on, learning that love ebbs and waxes but only dies if we neglect to cherish it."

"Is that . . ."

"How your father and I were? Of course. We were fortunate in our love, that we found one another. There was never such a splendid man as your father. He was so full of life he could raise other people's spirits just by walking into a room. I sometimes hear his laughter even now. It didn't seem possible to me that it could die, even if he did."

"I know," Maris said softly, a tear running down her cheek to nestle like a kiss on her lip.

"Yet, how at times I struggled to hold on to my patience. When he would bring the whole field home to dinner with no more notice than your coming with a message fifteen minutes before the rest were to arrive."

"I remember that," Maris said. "I'd never heard you swear before."

"'Blast' is hardly a swear word."

"That's not what you said. You said . . ."

Mrs. Lindel put her fingers over Maris's mouth. "I said 'blast.'"

"Yes, Mother," Maris said dutifully, her eyes alight.

"Your father was not always as tender of my feelings as he might have been, especially at first. He was still such a boy when we married. How my whims infuriated him! I was something of a flirt then, you see."

"You?"

"Why sound so amazed? I haven't always been comfortably plump, nor was my hair so gray. I think this year has aged me rather."

"I can't see it," Maris said, giving her mother's waist another squeeze.

"You're a good child. You won't make the mistakes I made. Do you know, at one time, I went running back to my mother, full of crochets and complaints about my brutal husband. My father was sympathetic—I was his darling which may have been half the problem. My mother, however, made no bones about it. If I had made a bad bargain, even after all my former raptures about this paragon, then it was up to me to put it right. So I went home again, only to find your father frantic with worry. I remember how long we talked, hours and hours into the night. Then I discovered you were coming along and there was nothing to do but stay together. In the end, we had more happiness than usually is granted to us poor mortals. I had him for nearly twenty years; more than most."

Maris knew that in another moment her mother would sniff, brush her hands together and find some task to do. Clinging to her for one sweet instant more, Maris dared to ask a question. "Is that why you look so faraway sometimes? You are thinking of the past?"

Her mother appeared startled. "Do I?"

"Sometimes."

"I can't guess what I would be thinking of. Whether Mrs. Cosby reminded the butcher to be more careful with his cutting, most likely." She seemed to realize that this flippant answer would not satisfy Maris. "Yes, I suppose I may fall into a reverie sometimes and that your father's time with me may well be the cause if I look sad. However, I hope I am enough of a Christian to believe that everything happens for . . . well, if not for the best, at least for a reason. As for my appearing somewhat pensive of late, one can hardly blame me."

"Because of what happened in London," Maris said, willing to assume this burden as well.

"London? Heavens, no. The world does not revolve about you, my dearest, not even my world. I have found myself wondering what I shall do once you and Sophie are married and living with your husbands."

"That day is farther off now than when I left for London," Maris said dryly.

"Farther off? Perhaps. Yet it will happen sooner or later; it's inevitable. Then what shall I do? I do not think I am of the temperament to merely sit by while I await the arrival of grandchildren."

"Then what?"

"I believe I will travel. I've always wished to see Italy and Constantinople."

Maris stared at her mother, wonderstruck. "You have?"

Mrs. Lindel laughed and pinched her daughter's cheek. "How little children know of their parents. Your father and I were supposed to go to France on our honeymoon but the Revolution made it unsafe. Then you were born and the situation on the Continent grew worse and worse. When the peace was declared in 1802, I couldn't go because Sophie was too young for me to leave her. Sometimes it seemed as though Napoleon came along just to spite my ambition. I find it very hard to forgive him for having been emperor for so long."

"How inconsiderate of him! May I come too, Mother? Italy sounds delightful and, if Constantinople pleases us, let us go on to the pyramids!"

"If you wish, my dear, of course. After you return from Bath, we shall see."

To everyone's surprise, Miss Menthrip made no objections to Lord Danesby sending her to Bath. She seemed to feel some distinction between burdening her friends with her troubles and accepting largesse from the lord of the manor.

She wrote him a letter of thanks, sometimes asking Maris for a word. "Seal that, my girl," she said. "I don't want him thinking that I have no gratitude."

"I'll send it off at once," Maris promised.

"See it's paid for. I owe him quite enough as it is without adding postage to the bill."

Maris carried away the standish and tray. After a moment's consideration, she wrote a postscript at the bottom of Miss Menthrip's letter, passing along her kind thought of saving his lordship the further expense of franking her letter. Maris thought it would amuse him.

Walking home through the bat-flitted twilight, Maris wondered if she would like Bath. She'd seen more of England in the last six months than in her entire lifetime before this spring. London had impressed her while Yorkshire had refreshed her admittedly battered spirit with its magnificent views.

Everyone who had journeyed to Bath had delightful tales to tell of its cultural and social spheres. Rational enjoyment seemed the order of the day, even for the valetundinarians trundled about in chairs to drink of and bathe in the famous waters. Maris felt a qualm of trepidation, however, whether these delights would be open or closed to a girl who had blotted her copybook as severely as she had, even though the fault stemmed from another's ambition.

There had been those in London who had cut her after the events at Durham House became public knowledge. It had seemed unfair that Mrs. Armitage should continue to be received, yet Maris felt this, too, was a valuable lesson. Even if the question of returning to town for another Season arose, she would debate the necessity until the idea was given up. Perhaps Sophie would have better fortune if her poet failed her. Maris would content herself for now with Bath.

"No matter what happens." She sighed. After all, she was not there to indulge in idle pleasures but to assist Miss Menthrip. Perhaps once she was entirely recovered, there would be time for other pursuits. Even if Maris were invited nowhere, there were supposed to be a great many public events, concerts and the like, open to subscribers.

"Another rented lodging." Maris sighed as they reached the town at last. It had been a slower journey than any she'd undertaken yet, for only a funereal pace would spare Miss Menthrip the worst of the bouncings and shakings inherent in travel by coach. Fortunately, the weather had continued fine, sparing them both mud and dust. The coach, though antiquated, was extremely roomy. Nevertheless, Maris felt overjoyed to be leaving it, stepping down into the shaded cool of late afternoon. She found herself in a quiet square, houses on all four sides, boxing in a small park in the center.

A large oak tree growing in the park extended its heavy branches as though stretching after a long sleep. Though some golden leaves dusted the street, the tree was still heavily laden enough to make an appreciable difference to the temperature. The square was so silent she could hear the rustle of the leaves as a treetop breeze toyed with them. The houses the tree shaded were all of red brick, yet there was sufficient difference in pediments, shutters, and frontispieces for the residents to tell one house from another.

Their own residence stood in the center of one side of the square, the sun sending its last rays over the roofs opposite to shine with dazzling brilliance on the windows above her. The door stood open, a man in the exquisitely correct clothes of the compleat butler advancing down the steps, two younger male servants following like acolytes. "Welcome, Miss Lindel. I am Tremlow, of the household."

Without any noticeable sign from him, the two footmen took their places beside the coach, one helping Miss Menthrip out, the other apparently prepared to sacrifice himself should she fall. "Your room awaits you, Miss Menthrip," Tremlow said. "Both tea and cordial will be sent up instantly."

"I don't deny I'll take them both and be glad." Though pale and unsteady on her feet, Miss Menthrip studied the butler with a sharp look. "Have I seen you before?"

"I don't believe so, madam." He bowed as she passed him. "If you'll accompany me, Miss Lindel?"

"Thank you." She followed him, marveling. He was nothing like the butler Mrs. Paladin had hired in London. One could not imagine soup stains on Mr. Tremlow's linen nor the slightest tinge of black under his fingernails. The very thought was an abomination.

The lower rooms that she glimpsed were furnished in an excellent style, modern without excess and touched with the occasional elegant antique. Since the lower rooms so exceeded the quality of those of the house in London, Maris assumed the private rooms were correspondingly even more shabby.

She found herself instead in the midst of a room so delicate and well planned that it seemed destined for some great lady. The vast bed's hangings were obviously French, rich, heavy tassels and silken ropes tying them back. Two large crystal vases stood on either side of the bed on gleaming tables, full of beautifully arranged flowers that scented the air like rare perfume. It reminded her briefly of the scent Lilah had spilled all those months ago.

Maris studied the butler. "As you have our names, I assume we are in the right house."

"Yes, Miss Lindel."

"By whom are you employed, Mr. Tremlow?"

"I was engaged by a firm of solicitors, miss. Messers Dewar, Pomfret, and Frears, Lincoln's Inn. They are also the agents for this house, which belongs to His Grace, the Duke of Saltaire." He made an adjustment to a window curtain as a lady's maid swept in, bearing a tray. The intoxicating smell of fresh china tea made Maris lick her dry lips in anticipation. "Will there be anything further, Miss Lindel?"

"No, thank you, Tremlow."

"Dinner will be served at your convenience, Miss Lindel."

"Thank you. Half an hour should suffice."

The house and the money had all been arranged through third and even fourth parties, in order to remove any impropriety from Lord Danesby's housing Miss Lindel. The fact that she was merely Miss Menthrip's companion would not have weighed against the fact of their earlier association. Not one person in a thousand would believe that she wasn't his mistress, Miss Menthrip's presence a mere blind, if the knowledge of who paid the rent should become disseminated.

Maris crossed the hall to visit Miss Menthrip and found her in bed, a very superior style of maidservant hanging up her clothes. "I shall press these few things, ma'am," she said with a curtsy as she bore off an armload of gowns.

"What in the name of all that's wonderful is the

meaning of this?" Miss Menthrip demanded when they were alone.

"Don't distress yourself."

"Distress myself? What's to be distressed about? I just don't understand what he thinks he is doing. I'm no fairy princess to be wafted to realms of gold at some sultan's wish."

"I certainly am not," Maris answered in reply to a certain expression in Miss Menthrip's coal black eyes. "To speak in earnest, ma'am, I believe it is simply that he ordered a house to be made ready in Bath and his solicitors undertook to do so. Perhaps they thought he himself meant to occupy the house. He wrote to Mother that everything would be done with the utmost discretion."

"Sounds fishy to me," Miss Menthrip said querulously. "I suspect that I'm the first person to ever lie upon this feather mattress. I further suspect that everything in this house is fresh from the joiners' hands."

"It certainly is elegant," Maris said. "Yet homelike as well. I wonder if the Duke who owns it spends much time in it."

"What duke?"

"The butler said this house belongs to the Duke of Saltaire, whoever he may be."

Miss Menthrip frowned and traced a curling vine embroidered on the coverlet. "Saltaire. It seems to me I've heard that name somewhere and recently too."

The doctor had warned Maris that sometimes after an illness an elderly person will suffer from gaps in their memory. He had every hope that Miss Menthrip's lapses would be short-lived, all the more reason not to make a fuss when she became forgetful.

"I'm sure I don't recall anyone by that name and I met hundreds of young men while in town."

"I hope you mean to tell me of all your conquests, Maris. I enjoyed your letters despite their being too short."

Maris laughed. "I broke very few hearts."

"More than you know, perhaps," Miss Menthrip said hopefully.

"I doubt it. I never knew any other man was even in the room. I had my eye fixed on an unobtainable pinnacle and lesser mortals hardly existed."

"Who?" Miss Menthrip breathed.

Maris realized she'd been speaking her thoughts aloud. Quickly, she turned aside Miss Menthrip's curiosity with a wave of her hand and a merry, "Why who else but the Prince Regent himself? Don't you know I simply dote on men of full habit? What should I do with a young buck with a head of thick hair and a trim waistcoat? A king or nothing for me."

"He won't be king for a good while yet, may it please God. You young things don't remember him when he was young and trim. The best-looking man in Europe, they called him once. Bath was a grand city then, not a creaking hospital. Mark my words, there won't be a soul under eighty at the baths tomorrow save for me and thee."

"Oh, surely not."

But Miss Menthrip wasn't listening to her. She had her head cocked to one side, the loose pewter gray braid falling free over her shoulder. "I hear wheels. Is it a visitor?"

"Surely not for us, ma'am. We shall have to grow

used to sharing visitors with our neighbors. In London it took me a long time to learn what to attend to and what to ignore."

Impossible, however, to ignore the rat-a-tat of the shining brass knocker on the front door. At Miss Menthrip's urging, Maris stepped out onto the landing and peered over the railing.

Tremlow's voice rose. "I shall ascertain, my lord, if you will wait."

Maris wished she'd done more than dab her face with a flannel and run a comb through her hair. She did not wish to meet Lord Danesby again looking as though she'd been dragged backward through a hedge. She hurried again into Miss Menthrip's room as the butler started up the stairs.

"His lordship has come to call," she gasped.

"Heavens, girl, no need to put yourself in such a taking. No doubt he's merely come to see how we fared on our journey. I call that gentlemanly to a fault. He could have just as well waited until tomorrow."

When Mr. Tremlow, bowing very low, bid Miss Menthrip to say whether she was at home to visitors, she assumed the grand manner as one who is born to it. Ignoring Maris's urgent signals from behind the butler to deny herself, she inclined her head graciously. "We should be pleased to see his lordship. Kindly request him to await us in the drawing room. We do have a drawing room?"

"Yes, Miss Menthrip. I shall inform him."

As soon as the door closed, she threw off her bedclothes and her invalidish air. "Go down at once, girl. First ring for that haughty wench. I've not the least notion where she put any of my clothes and I can't see Lord Danesby in this bed gown."

"You needn't see him," Maris said. "Pray don't agitate yourself; the doctor said it was bad for you."

"Pish! I'd not be here at all if it weren't for his lordship and I'll not turn him from my door the first night I'm here."

"He'd understand if you said you were too tired."

Miss Menthrip's wise dark eyes narrowed. "Are you certain it's not yourself who don't wish to see him? You can't be shy of him, not after making so bold as to call on him to beg his consideration for me."

"No, I'm not shy of him at all. I was merely thinking . . ."

"You think too much, Maris, that's half your complaint. Now, hurry along. Don't keep him waiting."

Maris reminded herself that she had no reason anymore to be shy of Lord Danesby. Her girlish idolatry of him was quite burnt out, replaced by a tentative liking, when she felt confident enough that liking was not in its way as great an impertinence as infatuation. That day at Finchley Place had confirmed her appreciation of his good qualities. He'd given her no reason to be either shy or embarrassed by any reference, even the most glancing, to what had occurred in town. His tall friend, Mr. Swift, had also been most gentlemanly, not only to her but to Lucy. She, poor thing, had been quite overcome by the company she'd found until both men, with great delicacy, had exerted themselves to put her at ease.

Despite her memories of their last meeting, Maris drew damp hands down her skirts just before entering the drawing room. Though this room was the most elegant she'd seen yet, she had no eyes for the moss green curtains or the delicately carved Chippendale furnishings. Lord Danesby rose to his feet on her entrance, and gave her his most enchanting smile.

"How good of you to call, my lord," she said, shaking hands.

He retained one in his clasp a moment to look at her most searchingly. She had almost to tug it free so that she could indicate he might be seated again.

"I need not ask if you find yourself well, Miss Lindel. Your pink cheeks tell me that tale."

She threw him a quizzical glance. "They lie. We have been but an hour out of the coach."

"Was it a difficult journey?"

"Not difficult, no. But long and slow. Ladies cannot tear about the countryside as you gentlemen do in your curricles and phaetons."

"I think you would look very dashing in a curricle, Miss Lindel. Shall I take you up in mine one morning? I should very much like to show you my cattle's paces."

"I should like that above all things, my lord." She rose and went to the bell. "We are about to partake of some supper, if you would care to join us?"

Kenton raised his hand to stop her. "I cannot stay. I merely came to assure myself that all was well. You like the house?"

"Very much, though the servants are rather grand personages."

With a sigh of relief, Kenton noted that her conversation had begun to take a much more "Maris" trend than the series of polite society nothings offered by every maiden. He'd realized at Finchley that only her appearance there had been unconventional. Once she returned from sponging the mud from her dress, she'd been impeccably correct.

When she had begun to pursue interesting side is-
sues, she had pulled herself up, as if someone had
whispered "propriety and dignity" in her ear. It had
worried him. He did not want her to lose her es-
pieglerie, that sense of the ridiculous that made her
such a darling.

"I can't imagine your going in terror of servants,"
he said, encouraging her.

"Oh, but you don't know how terrifying a very superior lady's maid can be."

"No, I don't. Though I remember taking great
care around my mother's dresser. Selby was her
name and her air of consequence would have been
excessive in a bishop."

She came back to sit down, leaning toward him.
"I've seen such women in the drapers' in town. One
would think their opinion of the dress lengths were
more important than their mistress's."

"At least you are spared the hauteur of the average gentleman's valet. I believe my man is generally
known as 'Napoleon the Second' below stairs."

She laughed softly, that delightful sound that
haunted his dreams. Yet, flatter himself to the top of
his bent, he could not persuade himself he saw anything in her eyes but friendship. She showed not
the slightest consciousness that he was a man and
she a woman, the appreciation of which was keeping him awake nights. Kenton longed to seize her in
his arms, but to slake selfishly his own need might
destroy the only good fortune he had—her liking of
him. He dared not risk a kiss, even though the gam-
ble might win him all.

Miss Menthrip entered before his conversational
skills broke down all together. After fifteen minutes,
during which they each took the other's fair mea-

sure, Kenton excused himself. "Nonsense; you'll stay to dinner. I've already told that high-nosed butler."

Controlling his smile at this description of his servant, Kenton made his apologies. "I mustn't stay. Another time, perhaps."

Miss Menthrip nodded, the edges of the lace square pinned to her head fluttering. "You'd better go tell him, Maris, or he'll be in a taking."

"Yes, ma'am. Good evening, my lord. Thank you again for coming to see how we are."

Kenton had not for one moment assumed he'd leave this house without a private word from Miss Menthrip. She was no fluffy-minded spinster, easily charmed by a title and polished address. For that reason alone, he was glad it was she chaperoning Maris. There were not many young men in Bath at this season but there were a few dancing attendance on invalid relations or *malade imaginaires* with fortunes to leave. Let them catch a glimpse of a beauty like Maris and they'd cluster around. He was glad Miss Menthrip would be there to ward off even the most lustrous among them. Or would she?

"I'm not to call? Ever?"

"I'm sorry, my lord, but I think it's wisest. If Maris is ever to have a chance at a husband, Mrs. Lindel and I think it best if she no longer associates with a man so involved in her near ruination. We know, of course, that it wasn't your fault, nor hers."

"Surely, however, if I'm not allowed to speak with her, that will give rise to more rumors than if we continue to meet socially." Kenton tried to keep from revealing his emotions, something no proper Englishman should have had any trouble repressing. This sharp-eyed spinster seemed to have some sympathy, though for whom, Maris or himself, he could not tell.

"Well, I shan't throw myself in front of her if you choose to speak to her at an assembly or even dance with her. But for Maris's sake, for the sake of her future, she must have the chance to meet other men. Men who have not been found alone with her in a bedchamber in the middle of the night."

Put that way, "for Maris's sake," he could find no objection. The idea of Maris finding another man, however, brought out all his objections, cut and long-tail. "In time, I assure you, this half-born scandal will be forgotten. Worse sins have been forgotten in no time at all. Another scandal arises and the details of the former one become indistinct to the point of vanishment."

"As the sister of a history scholar, I am aware of the temporary nature of scandal. The matter takes on a different cast when the focus of the defamation is a girl one has known from her childhood. I would have nothing further touch her happiness."

Kenton nodded. This he not only understood but endorsed completely. "Very well. I shall not visit here again."

Maris returned to them. He saw her smile tremble and fade as she sensed the tension between her friend and . . . her other friend. Kenton wanted to bring the pleasurable light back to her face. He excused himself and stepped out into the hall.

When he came back, he bore in his hands the welcome present he'd brought for her. Maris came close to him, her eyes fixed on the glossy green leaves, the edges tinged with soft red. With one finger, she caressed the half-furled petals of the single bud. She smiled up into his eyes. "You shouldn't give me this. You said you only received twelve plants from Mr. Chavez."

"It's terribly tiny," Miss Menthrip said. "I'm sure it will be a fine specimen when it grows."

"It's a miniature rosebush," Maris answered. "From Monserrat. Isn't it beautiful? It came so far and now it's mine." Kenton looked into Maris's eyes and saw the glint of a rose fancier being born. "Will you tell me how to care for it?"

"I wrote down some instructions," he said, pulling them from his pocket. The papers had ruined the fit of his coat but he hadn't minded. "Keep it the same temperature as you yourself find comfortable and it should thrive."

She nodded. Looking over her shoulder at her friend, she said, "Tremlow tells me our dinner is ready. Won't you precede me? I should like his lordship to explain the care of this plant."

"Another time," Kenton said, obedient to the indulgent but warning glance of her preceptress.

"Tomorrow?"

"You mustn't tease his lordship," Miss Menthrip said, and Maris at once acquiesced.

"No. You've been far too kind already."

He could have stayed and disputed his kindness if their dinner had not been waiting. Kenton took his leave. Maris went with him to the door and shook hands in a most friendly fashion. The only comfort he took from this good-bye was that at least she didn't treat him like an uncle.

"That went well," Miss Menthrip said briskly.

Maris listened for the closing of the door, the rosebush in its diminutive terra-cotta pot still in her hands. "What did he say when you told him my mother's wishes?"

"Nothing very much. He seemed to understand the necessity and to approve of her caution."

Maris longed to ask for every detail of the conversation she had missed. Not in any infatuated way but only because his lordship had been kind to her often and she did not wish to offend him. She doubted he would feel any loss at being forbidden to call on a girl who, in addition to nearly trapping him into marriage, had a fatal tendency to say the wrong thing. "He didn't seem offended? I shouldn't wish him to feel that his company is repugnant."

"No, he showed no particular feeling at all. He behaved just as a gentleman ought. It is not their way to suffer from an excess of emotion. My brother used to say a man should know neither the heights nor the depths of emotion, that all that should be left to the women."

"Do you agree?" Maris asked, putting the rosebush down on a crocheted doily on the pianoforte.

"Agree?" Miss Menthrip echoed blankly.

"Yes. Do you agree with your late brother's assessment of men and women?"

"I'm sure he must have been correct. He was a most notable scholar, you know."

"So I have heard. Come, we had better go to dinner now or we shall be in great disgrace with our new servants." Maris cast a last glance back at the jaunty little rosebush, its single bud standing up proudly. She wondered what the last Professor Menthrip would have made of such a gift. She wondered what Lord Danesby meant by it—friendship, admiration, or farewell?

Chapter Thirteen

Miss Menthrip showed no reluctance when it came to following her doctor's orders. As soon as she was dressed, she wanted Maris to accompany her to the Pump Room, where glasses of the hot water were served out by liveried footmen. The water itself hardly deserved the sumptuous early Georgian surroundings or the black-patined dolphin fountains from which it flowed. Murky, scummed, and smelling like a mad alchemist's favorite preservative for alligator, the water may have done little for a laundry list of complaints, but it certainly built fortitude.

After writing her name and address in the book kept for that purpose, Miss Menthrip resolutely gulped down a glassful, declaring, "I can feel it having a powerful effect already."

Another lady, hardly in her first youth despite her foaming muslin gown, overheard. "It's remarkably fine water," she said in a breathless voice. "Better than Malvern or Leamington."

"Have you been to those places?" Miss Menthrip asked with interest.

"Oh, yes, indeed. My mother is a sad invalid, you see, and I have grown accustomed to attending her at the various spas. Is this your daughter?" she asked, turning a pair of pale blue, vaguely curious eyes toward Maris.

Miss Menthrip denied it and the two ladies fell into a natural conversation. Maris, bored but resigned, began observing the others present. A string quartet played quietly in one corner. The Pump Room was quite sunny this morning, though it had been raining off and on all night, giving even the oldest patients the illusion of warmth and health. Maris was looking on in considerable amusement as one tiny but imperious lady in a wheeled chair ordered no less than three hulking attendants about like so many chess pieces, when she thought she heard her name called.

Miss Menthrip, still deep in conversation with the faded lady, hadn't called her. Maris looked around, a small hope kindling in her heart that it might be Lord Danesby. Surely, however, he'd not wish to see her after receiving her mother's ruling last night. Maris knew it was for her own good not to see his lordship, though that made it no easier to have refused a friend.

"Miss Lindel, isn't it?" A young man bowed before her, his coat a trifle too tight around his middle. A good-humored round face smiled up at her, waiting for recognition. A memory stirred.

"Sir Rigby Barrington, is it not? What brings you to Bath, sir?"

He nodded down the room. "M'mother's taken a fancy to drink the waters, though myself I think it's more the whist and the theater that drew her."

"Which lady is your mother, sir?" She followed the direction of his gaze and hid a smile as she realized it was the tiny empress all in inky black.

"That's her. The Holy Terror." Sir Rigby was smiling fondly as he said it. "Indomitable Irene."

"You shouldn't speak of her so to me," Maris said, choking a little on a laugh.

Sir Rigby grinned, rendering himself even more youthful. "You'll like her. She's corking."

"I'm sure I would."

"Come and meet her."

"Thank you, Sir Rigby, but I am with a friend."

"You wouldn't send me back alone, Miss Lindel? She sent me to ask you to be introduced, you know, and I daren't for my life go back without you."

"Yes," Maris said, smiling at him. "I can see you go about in a perfect panic of her displeasure."

She remembered Sir Rigby in town as being someone who aped the manners and dress of more notable gentlemen, running through the catalog from starched shirt points at his eye, too many fobs across a round stomach, and extremely dressy boots. He had sent her flowers, she recalled, after her first ball, though she had not danced with him. Later, they had met on several occasions. He'd proved to be remarkably light on his feet, one of the best dancers she'd ever stood up with.

In Bath, his desire to take the wind out of every dandy's eye had been checked. He wore the plain but neat dress of a gentleman who was not yet top o'the trees and who might yet resign himself to never gaining that pinnacle. Yet his natural good humor, which had shone through even extravagant dress, seemed even more evident now.

Maris introduced Sir Rigby to Miss Menthrip, who raised no objection to her charge going the length of the Pump Room with a young man.

"Is this your first visit to Bath, Miss Lindel?" he asked.

"Yes, my friend was ill for a time and we have hopes the water may aid her in recovering her strength."

"It's a wonder to me how these venerable folks come back here year and year. Look, there's old General Sir Ogden Macafeeny making a beeline for Mama. Ninety-two if he's a day and still the most desperate flirt in town."

"Thank you for the warning," Maris said.

"Ha, you laugh now. But I've seen the old dog woo and win too many times. I wish I might study his strategy."

"If he wishes to speak with your mother, perhaps we should not intrude."

"Never mind. If Mama wants to see you, old beaus will have to go to the wall. Sons, too, more than likely."

He did not seem crushed by his mother's curt request to "take himself off" when he'd introduced Miss Lindel to her. Maris noted he did not go far enough to be out of earshot. Though Lady Barrington's hands might tremble and her movements might be stiff, her small black eyes were not dimmed by age or by sentiment. Her ivory white face floated above the rich black she wore for her son, killed in Spain. Her voice creaked like a parrot's. "You're that chit who nearly trapped Danesby."

Maris judged that this was a deliberate goad to see how she would jump. "Yes, ma'am. Alas that my strategy failed," she said, casting her gaze toward the decorated ceiling in a parody of hypocritical rue.

"Alas, indeed, if you think me gulled by such nonsense. It was Elvira Paladin's plot as I very well know.

What are you doing in Bath? Come to lick your wounds?"

"Had I any, I should wish to bathe them, but I have none."

"What? Not one regret at losing a fine title, a grand fortune, and a handsome husband all in one moment? I hear you turned him down flat."

"What good is a title and fortune if your handsome husband despises you for tricking him into marriage, ma'am?"

"Ha, there speaks a starry-eyed babe. Don't trouble to deny it. All girls are romantic until they outgrow it." One bony finger crooked, drawing Maris nearer. "Men never do outgrow it. Look at that foolish boy of mine. Denying me grandchildren until he 'falls in love.' Bah! I've no patience with that sort of lunacy."

Sir Rigby turned around at this, though Lady Barrington didn't see him. He winked at Maris, then was taken aback when she returned the gesture. After a moment, he grinned.

"Sir Rigby is very engaging," Maris said. "I'm sure he'll soon give you all you want."

"An optimist, too? Who's that woman with whom you entered the Pump Room."

"A Miss Menthrip, ma'am, from my hometown of Finchley."

"That's right. I'd heard you'd known Danesby before you'd come to town. The two of you may call on me later today." She reached out with the stick that lay beside her knee and nudged one of her attendants in the back. The large man turned, nothing but the most ardent concern on his face. "I'm ready to go. Rigby, you see Miss Lindel home."

With Lady Barrington's support, Maris and Miss

Menthrip found Bath to be socially quite the equal
of London. Miss Menthrip's dry humor soon made
her a favorite of her ladyship. The baron's widow
and the scholar's sister found they had little in common besides a general distrust of the manners and
morals of youth, their own friends and relations ex-
empt from the strictures laid on the rest of mortals
under thirty. This was enough to cement a lifelong
friendship.

Despite the pace of balls, at-home impromptus,
and visits to the theater, Miss Menthrip looked
younger every week. Even the steep hills of the town
didn't seem to distress her, though Maris often
wished she would take a chair when she walked up
to the Crescent to visit the Barringtons. "I'm well
enough," she said, taking a deep breath of the fresh
air rising from the river. "If the lease on the house
weren't for four more weeks, I could go home tomorrow feeling more rested than I have in years."

"It is not your health that troubles me," Maris
said, leaning her gloved hand against one of the pil-
lars of creamy golden stone that proliferated
throughout the city. "It's my own. I can't keep up."

"You young people have no stamina. Though I
noticed when we went shopping the other day, you
had no wish to rest."

"That's different," Maris said loftily. "Besides, we
weren't purchasing, and that makes all the difference. Nothing is more exhausting than buying."

"I still argue in favor of that brown silk bonnet
with the long ribbons," Miss Menthrip said, then
caught her breath with a gasp. "Oh, look. Is that
Lord Danesby? No. Or is it?" She peered shortsightedly down the street, then fluttered her
handkerchief, having made up her mind.

Maris saw him raise a hand in greeting, then begin to cross the street to come to them. She felt the old tremulous excitement in her breast and scolded herself. There was no need for this fervency. That was an old reaction, left over from when she adored him. True, he'd been in her dreams nearly every night, she reflected, preparing a smile of greeting. But a girl could not be held responsible for anything but her daydreams.

She hadn't seen him for three days, not since he'd danced with her at a subscription ball in the lower rooms. They'd apparently resumed quite their old footing, she thought, though he hadn't seemed to care for Sir Rigby, declaring him to be an overfed popinjay. Maris had defended him, saying that his clothing was far more tasteful in Bath than in town. His plumpness was not his fault, as it worried his mother if he lost any weight or even ate less.

Now as he lifted his curly brimmed hat to them, she smilingly gave him her hand. "I had hoped to see you on Saturday, Lord Danesby. You had said that you would help me understand the play."

"I'm sure your friends assisted you," he said crisply.

"If you mean Sir Rigby, he has no head for Shakespeare. Fortunately, Miss Menthrip's brother had made quite a hobbyhorse of him and she could help me unravel *As You Like It*."

"And did you?"

"Very much so."

"Sir Rigby would make an excellent student of Shakespeare, if he attended more closely," Miss Menthrip said thoughtfully. "Do you recall how he wished he might have a Rosalind to teach him how to woo in form? I thought that showed he was attending."

"He needs no further tutelage in that subject," Maris said gaily.

"Are you going to the Crescent now?" Lord Danesby asked, his voice dark.

"Miss Menthrip is," Maris answered. "Our ways part here. I have a bonnet to buy."

"May I offer you my escort, Miss Menthrip?" he asked.

Maris smiled to see him offer his arm in the grand style. Miss Menthrip, however, seemed at a loss, glancing between the two younger people. "I warn you, my lord," Maris said, "Miss Menthrip takes no rest between the Bridge and the Crescent. She seems to think it un-British to do so."

"I shall not cry a halt before she does so."

"Yes, you will," Maris said with a laugh. "Good day."

Kenton watched Maris walk away, her parasol open above her head, her carriage very upright yet with a lightness that made it a definite effort not to follow her. Two middle-aged bucks on the strut paused to look after her, one raising a quizzing glass, and Kenton frowned. "When may I wish her happy?" he asked Miss Menthrip curtly.

"I cannot say. Not soon, I think."

"Not soon? Do you mean that Barrington has been trifling with her? Surely he must mean marriage."

"I cannot say," Miss Menthrip repeated. "If he has given her any sign of affection, I have not seen it."

"She would tell you, I'm sure," Kenton said, still

distracted. If that second buck turned back to follow Maris, he would know how to act.

"I'm not sure she would. Maris has changed, my lord. She has not quite the open, confiding nature I saw in her when she was a girl."

"London changed that, soon enough."

"And do you bear no part in that change?" Miss Menthrip asked.

"Too much for my peace of mind, ma'am."

"So I see," she muttered but Kenton only heard her vaguely. The second buck had taken one step after Maris but his friend had apparently reminded him of an appointment. Kenton's fists relaxed.

"I tell you this, my lord. If he asks and she accepts it will not be for love on either side."

"I beg your pardon? When they have all but been living in each other's pockets for weeks. Half the town is certain they are in love."

"The less gossips know, the more they say," Miss Menthrip said sharply. "I have been living in Maris's pocket, as you put it, and I know the truth. They are more like brother and sister than Rosalind and Orlando. If he asks her to marry him, it will be because his mother has dinned it into his ears how much she likes Maris."

"Does she?"

"Immensely, but then, she'd love any girl that boy brought home as a bride. If by some chance she didn't, the first infant would change her mind."

"And why would Maris marry him?" he said, like a man worrying a sore tooth, knowing it will be agony but unable to keep from exploring. "Because he's rich?"

Miss Menthrip snorted. "If Maris were mercenary, she'd be married to you."

He looked down at her, forgetting for an instant to shield his feelings behind armor. When she blinked and stammered, he realized she'd seen the truth. "I wish to God she were mercenary," he said.

She patted his forearm. "Why don't you ask her, my lord?"

He shook his head, her sympathy no solace. "She wouldn't have me when she was in love with me. She wouldn't have me now."

"She might. She's so lonely."

"Lonely? Maris?" He looked down the street, but she had slipped into a shop or otherwise gone out of sight. "I thought she was enjoying Bath. I see her or hear of her everywhere."

"Pish. What good are parties and such? She doesn't laugh as she used to. The only time I hear her really laugh is when she's with you."

The hope he'd been keeping alive with half-glimpsed sightings of her and the occasional dance burned a little stronger at this. But he couldn't accept it. "Has she told you that she isn't in love with Barrington?"

"Not in so many words," Miss Menthrip said.

"Then she may be."

"And pigs may fly." She gave the arm she still held a little shake. "Don't be a fool. Go after her. Ask her. She's in Madame Emelie's shop, meeting her maid. Ask her to walk with you in the Gardens. Ask her."

He nodded once and set off down the street. The street turned into a bridge, though one couldn't tell as shops lined it so that one could only see the river by going into the back of one of the shops. Yet Pulteney Bridge was one of his favorite sights in Bath. He hoped they'd never pull it down as they had

London Bridge, for it had always meant Bath to
him. Now, it might always mean Maris. He hurried.

The maid was there, chatting with the assistant.
Maris had gone. The maid, one of his own from
Finchley, blanched white as muslin when she recognized him. She could only stammer when
questioned. Fortunately, the shopgirl was made of
sterner stuff. "The gentleman said they should walk
in the Gardens to discuss matters." Her voice was
more refined than that of most of the duchesses he
knew.

"What gentleman?" Kenton demanded, confused
by this new note of masculinity.

"Oh, I know, my lord," his maid said. "It was that
Sir Rigby Barrington. He's called ever so often."

He handed them each the first two coins he met
with in his pocket and rushed out.

He hurried down Great Pulteney Street toward
the Sydney Gardens, a great oval at the end. Kenton
didn't know why he felt such a sense of urgency. He
could propose to Maris at any time, surely, choosing
his moment for the best outcome. Yet here he was,
racing along, giving the cut direct to at least two
friends, all to catch up with her and interrupt her
tête-à-tête with a man described as "more like a
brother than a lover."

Yet when he found them at last, he did not interrupt.

They stood no more than a breath apart in the
shelter of one of the little antique follies that stood
among the trees. The dry autumn tints of amber
and gold made a background like tapestry work behind them. Maris listened, her eyes cast down, while
Sir Rigby puffed a stream of words into the air. He
held both her hands in his own.

Kenton had been sure that he loved Maris from the moment she'd turned him down at Durham House. Every time he'd seen her since, the feelings he had discovered grew stronger. He wanted to cherish her, to defend her, but at the same time encourage her to grow into the kind of woman her destiny decreed. He didn't want to keep her in a box, preserved in youth and folly. He wanted to share all the joys and miseries of her life by her side. He'd thought he loved her as much as any man could love the partner of his heart.

Yet, seeing her now, listening to the protestations of some other lover saying the words that were his, he knew he had not loved her at all. Watching her shake her head and then, after another spate of words, nod, smiling into another man's eyes, Kenton felt a pain as though his heart had been cut in two with one brutal stroke. What was left, rising like a phoenix from the ashes, proved to be a truer love yet. He still longed for her. However, if she felt Sir Rigby was the man for her, then he would not interfere with that choice. It was the gift of a true lover to his beloved—the understanding that she belonged ultimately to herself, not to him.

Kenton stepped back into the shelter of the trees, where he could wipe quickly under his eyes without anyone seeing. By some shift in the wind or acoustics, he could now hear the deeper tones of Sir Rigby's voice, if not Maris's.

"It's settled then. You'll come. You'll definitely come?"

She nodded again, her lips moving silently.

"Tonight, then. You'll be able to sneak away?"

What was this? Kenton stared at them, wishing he dared come closer. They couldn't be planning to elope? Not with Lady Barrington having planned her son's wedding down to every detail, excepting the name of the bride.

"It'll be wonderful. You're such a Trojan, Maris. I can't thank you enough."

This did not sound like the language of a successful wooer. Kenton strained forward, striving to hear more. He caught just the thread of Maris's voice. "I wouldn't do it for any other man."

Kenton stayed hidden until they'd gone away. Then he sat down on the steps of their folly to think. If it was an elopement, perhaps to escape Lady Barrington's sway, then the worst turn he could serve her would be to put a spoke in their wheel. Sir Rigby was well-to-do; Maris would want for nothing. He was a mild-tempered, pleasant chap whom she might even grow to love. Thinking of Maris gazing at Sir Rigby with the same glow in her eyes she'd once had for him, Kenton dropped his head into his hands and groaned.

However, he thought, and brightened, if Rigby has some nefarious plot in mind, thinking Maris has already lost her virtue, then he must find some way of stopping it.

The best plan, he decided, would be to watch the house and follow them. If their path led to a chaise and team bound on a northward road, all well and good, for their destination would be Scotland. If Rigby hired only a pair and went any direction but north, Sir Rigby would very soon find himself laid out for his funeral, not his wedding.

It was dark under the great tree in the square as Kenton stood by, his horse's reins passed under his arm. There had been some delay in acquiring his horse from the stables where his cattle resided, and he now feared that he might have missed Maris altogether. On the way out of the Gardens, they may have made some more definite appointment than merely "tonight."

In the end, he had only to wait half an hour, but it seemed far longer. The mellow chiming of Bath Abbey's bells over the old stone city gave the quarter hour as a chaise and *pair* rolled up in front of the house. Sir Rigby leaped down, then stopped and looked anxiously at the horses.

Apparently he was expected, for Tremlow did not ask him to wait. As he passed in, he said, "I say, do you hear a funny noise?"

"Of what category, Sir Rigby?"

"Sort of a grinding noise. I thought it was my horse but it was a damn funny sound for a horse to make, unless it's got something wrong with its teeth."

"I know little of horses, Sir Rigby. They have not often fallen within my sphere."

What was Tremlow doing being so chatty? Kenton expected his butler to be as taciturn at this square as he was at Finchley. There, his sense of consequence hardly permitted him to speak to Kenton, let alone a young man calling upon a lady of the house.

Within fifteen minutes, the door opened again and both Sir Rigby and Maris came out. No bandbox or valise encumbered either of them. Kenton frowned anew, feeling that the lines in his forehead would never smooth again. Maris couldn't imagine she was going as far as Gretna without a change of clothing. What if she thought she was only going on a short jaunt, but Rigby meant to abduct her? Or perhaps she was a willing participant in whatever scheme was afoot.

Kenton wished he had a flask with him. Instead, he decided to stop making wild surmises and stick to the facts he could observe.

With a creak of the saddle leather, Kenton followed the chaise. It wasn't hard; Rigby wasn't much of a whip and his job horses were the sort of great slugs palmed off on such undiscerning men. Kenton's only difficulty lay in holding his own horse to such a halting pace.

His first fact was a simple one. They crossed the Avon to the south over the old Bath Bridge. No Gretna Green this trip. The new Wells and Westminster road rang beneath his hooves and he dropped back so the fugitives couldn't hear.

He didn't know the southern routes so well as the ones to the east, and his concentration was focused forward rather than to either side. They kept a fairly straight road, always heading slightly south and west. Only about five miles had been covered, taking hardly any time at all, even when matching his pace to Rigby's caution, when the chaise drew into the courtyard of a small inn. Kenton could see over the wall that surrounded the inn yard from horseback.

"We shan't be more than an hour," Rigby said to the ostler.

Maris had halted on the threshold to hear this, yet still showed no signs of alarm. Whether she had chosen Rigby out of loneliness or love, Kenton couldn't stand by any longer. Not to interfere in her choice of husband was one thing; to make no shift to stop her headlong slide into ruination was quite another. He owed his interference to her mother as well as to herself.

He dismounted and tossed the reins to the ostler's boy. "I shall be somewhat less than an hour," he growled as he strode into the inn.

"Quality," the ostler said with a shrug.

Chapter Fourteen

The inn's hall was dark and smoky, lit only by a lamp glowing on a table at the entrance. From behind one of the doors came a noise as of many merry people gathered together. A memory of another such hall flickered through Kenton's mind, but he had neither the time nor the inclination to track the impression to its source.

A heavyset woman, her low-cut gown filled in with a many-pleated lace tucker, passed at the end of the hall, a branch of candles held high in her hand. "Yes, sir?" she said, spying him.

"I've a message for the young lady who just arrived."

"Young lady? Would that be the Spanish madam?"

"No. This one's English. She drove up not ten minutes ago."

"Indeed, sir. With the young gentleman?"

"Yes," Kenton said, controlling himself. "With the young . . . gentleman."

Her experienced eye ran over him, appraising boots, coat, and cut. She put the candles on the table and wiped her hands on the pinafore that covered her dress. "It's not an elopement, is it? My man's very strong against this eloping. We had a runaway couple from Exmouth pass through here last year and I've only just heard the end of it from Mr. Ponsonby. I'd not want to be stirring him up again."

He forced a laugh. "No, indeed it's not an elopement. May I see the young lady?"

"What name shall I say?"

"She wouldn't know it. I've been chasing her since she left town with a message. From her mother."

"Ah, her mother, is it?" Mrs. Ponsonby's large mouth unfolded in a smile. "This way, sir. Such a taking thing," she said, picking up her candles. "Every other word is 'If you please' and 'If it's not too much trouble.' Not like that Spanish one, ordering me about like a slave. If it weren't it being the slow time of year, I'd have turned her out."

Kenton wasn't listening. He tried to plan what he would say to Maris, as he'd tried on the road. All his speeches fell through before his overwhelming curiosity as to what she thought she was doing.

"Here's a gentlemen to see you, miss," the landlady said, opening the door to the coffee room.

"Yes?" Maris said, turning away from the fire. For a moment, her eyes still dazzled from the flames, all she could see was a tall shadow, his riding coat sweeping the floor as he entered. The door closed behind him.

"What in the name of God do you think you are doing?" he demanded.

"Kenton?" Her hand flew to the base of her throat. "I beg your pardon. Lord Danesby, how came you here?"

He swept toward her, throwing his hat aside. She caught one glimpse of his face, hard, set, his eyes brilliant, before he clasped her against his body.

With one hand, he pushed her chin up, none too gently, and then he kissed her.

Shock held her rigid but nearly as quick and far stronger came delight. She didn't know how to kiss him in return, though in dreams she often had. Surely, though, she could do more than just stand here while he made all the effort.

At the first intimation of her struggle to get her hands free, he misinterpreted her move and let her go. Maris pressed her fingers to her lips, hardly believing what had happened. She shut her eyes tightly, sure that when she opened them, he'd vanish like the figment of her imagination he must be. One moment, she'd been waiting for Rigby to return and the next she was being unmercifully kissed by Kenton. Perhaps there'd been a carriage accident she didn't recall and she was at present lying somewhere either unconscious or under opiates. She didn't care how badly she was hurt so long as this hallucination held.

Kenton paced several times up and down in front of the fireplace. Her eyes dwelling on him in loving amazement, she saw that he wore riding dress and his boots were rather dusty. His hair was more disarranged than she'd ever seen it. She wanted to smooth it down, especially the one twist that rose from the back of his head.

He came to her and took her hands. "Maris, I swear I'll never ask you again what you are doing here with Barrington. But I must ask you to come back to Bath with me now."

"Back to Bath? But yes, that's where we're going."

"In an hour? Are you worth no more time to him than that?"

Now she was even more confused. "You may not

ask me what I am doing here, Lord Danesby, but I must ask you. Unless the Coachwheel is your usual evening haunt?"

"Hardly," he said with a twist of his lips. "I overheard you and Barrington talking in the Sydney Gardens this afternoon."

"Oh, I see. No. You couldn't have possibly thought this an assignation, which I assume you are hinting, if you overheard us there."

"I only heard part."

His clasp on her hands had gradually loosened, rather to her disappointment. Now he released them, and leaned his elbow on the mantelpiece. She saw that the laughter had come back into his eyes. That was a relief, but at the same time, she had thrilled to the blazing brilliance she'd seen there just before he'd kissed her. She'd been unable to interpret that look then. Now she could hardly wait to see it again.

"Start at the beginning, Maris. If you please."

"It's very simple. Three years ago, Rigby went to Spain to visit his younger brother."

"During the war?"

"Yes. His brother was stationed in Barcelona—is that the right word? Stationed?"

"What does Barrington's travels have to do with you being here alone with him?" Kenton asked.

"I'm not alone with him; I'm alone with you," she said saucily. For an instant, she thought she saw that blaze again as he straightened. She decided, as he once more assumed his relaxed pose, that it had merely been a reflection from the firelight.

"At any rate, Rigby went to Barcelona and there he met a girl. To hear him speak, one would think

she is an angel from heaven but to hear the landlady tell it, I have my doubts."

"The 'Spanish madam'? You mean the girl is
here?"

"Yes, upstairs. Rigby went up to her not fifteen
minutes ago, though I think he rather underesti-
mated the time necessary for a reunion. They have
been parted for so long, you see."

"Did he marry her in Spain?"

"Yes. It was quite the romance, though sadly they
were separated soon after they were wed. He didn't
know if she was alive or dead until just a few months
ago."

"Most touching," he said dryly. He shook his
head, disarranging his dark hair even more. A stray
lock fell over his forehead and Maris's fingers itched
to brush it back. "I cannot picture Rigby Barrington
wooing and winning a Spanish beauty. Even if he
did, how do you come into it? He never drove you
here at this hour of the night to meet his wife."

"But he did. She only arrived today. He is hoping,
as his mother quite likes me, that I can give Yolanda
a few hints on how to please her. I told him that the
mere fact of his marriage should be enough, but he
doesn't believe me. You see, his brother died in
Spain and he's afraid Lady Barrington will hold that
against his wife."

"This is the greatest rigmarole I've ever heard in
my life," Kenton said. "Lady Barrington is more
likely to fall on the girl's neck than turn her from
the door."

"That's what I thought," Maris said, an uncontrollable chuckle on her lips. "Poor Rigby. I fear
he'll never know another moment's peace. I
couldn't refuse him; he painted such a touching

picture of his poor little lost bride, all alone in a great strange country."

Kenton nodded. "The man's a romantic fool. Unless she was wafted across the sea by angels, she must have managed quite well on her own."

"I believe he spared no expense once she was located."

That seemed to dispose of Sir Rigby Barrington's affairs. The memory of Kenton's entrance and the kiss hung between them. Maris glanced up into his face. Finding him studying her, she found the fire fascinating once again.

"Maris . . ." he said quietly. "I'm not going to apologize."

"I didn't ask you to. You . . . you had your reasons, no doubt." The expectant quivering in her heart spread to her whole body. Could she be such a fool as to allow her feelings for him to reanimate?

"Yes, I had. They were good reasons. Would you care to hear them?" She didn't care what his reasons were, so long as they still held true. "I couldn't let you throw yourself away on a popinjay like Barrington. I know how lonely you must be, Maris, but don't choose a mate because of that."

"How did you know I was lonely?" she asked wonderingly. "I didn't think anyone guessed."

His smile held all the tenderness she'd dreamed of. "I'm lonely too. I never realized how much I needed you until you refused my offer at Durham. I didn't propose because of that nonsense with Mrs. Paladin. You didn't believe me then but I was so happy that I'd been handed that chance. It made me see the truth."

"What truth?" she asked, wanting him to stop talking and wishing he would go on.

He reached out and gathered her in, hands, shoulders, waist. "That I'd fallen in love with you the first time I saw you, laughing in St. Paul's."

Borne away on the bliss of Kenton's embrace, she did not think it necessary that he'd seen her once before that and had not found her at all prepossessing. Perhaps she'd tell him about that some other time, or perhaps not.

"Did you?"

"I must have," he said, kissing the corner of her mouth, right on the dimple. "I cannot imagine why else I would have suffered such a sudden revulsion of feeling at the thought of continuing with Flora Armitage. The only element that had changed was your presence there."

Standing this close to him, cradled against his chest, Maris could smile at his previous association. "How do you usually break off your connections?"

"With delicacy and tact. But you needn't worry. There won't be any more."

"So if you suddenly become terribly tactful, I should have a care." The immediate tightening of his arms and the gratifying roughness of his kiss relieved her mind. This time, she had her hands free and felt a wild new sense of freedom as she slipped her hands shyly about his neck, smoothing the wayward lock of hair at the back of his head. His hair was thick and soft. She ran a finger over the edge of his ear and down his throat, so different from her own.

His voice grew gruff. "Maris. I'm in love with you."

"Yes," she said dreamily, lifting her chin for another kiss.

He gave it to her, then, putting his hands to her

shoulders, he pushed her back an inch. Maris rocked slightly on her heels, opening her eyes. His smile was half amused, half eager. "Maris, did you hear me?"

"Of course," she said, trying to move in again but his strong forearms were braced against her.

"What do you say to that?"

She paused. "Thank you?"

"Maris," he said, the twinkle in his eyes fading. "Without sounding like a popinjay, I know you loved me once . . ." He stopped when she shook her head, his hands dropping slowly away, as though cherishing this last instant of contact.

Maris smoothed her own hair back from her forehead, her coiffure having unaccountably begun to loosen. "I never loved you, Kenton. That wasn't love. It was a mixture of hero worship, immaturity, and self-preservation. I wasn't about to risk falling in love with someone who might love me back. Much too frightening."

"I understand," he said. Kenton stepped back, folding his arms across his chest as though holding some pain at bay.

"No, you don't." Maris pushed him gently into the big armchair beside the fire and sank down on her knees beside him. "I didn't fall in love with you—with *you*, Kenton Danesby, not some imaginary, untouchable prince—until we met in London. You were so approachable, so friendly. I felt happy whenever we met. Then you became so entangled in that woman's plotting that I couldn't help feeling sorry for you. Something, by the way, the great and noble Lord Danesby never made me feel. *He* never needed anyone's help or fell into any difficulties from which he could not instantly extricate himself.

But you needed me, if only to refuse to marry you when all the world seemed to demand it."

"And now, Maris?" Kenton said, grasping her hand and pulling her up onto his lap. "What now?"

Breathless and trembling after a kiss wherein she gave as much as she received, Maris whispered, "Whatever you want, Kenton."

"I think we should be married, don't you?"

"Gretna Green? We could borrow Rigby's chaise."

Kenton pulled another pin from his beloved's hair. "We owe it to the *ton* to be married as ostentatiously as possible."

"With two marchionesses to hold up my train," Maris murmured. "But I'll settle for doves."

"Whatever you want, my darling."

Half an hour later, still ensconced together in the big armchair, they heard a commotion on the stairs. A baby was crying lustily, a woman was speaking very rapidly in a foreign tongue while another woman defended herself in far from parliamentary tones. Every now and again a voice unmistakably Rigby Barrington's broke in, throwing conciliatory clichés into the storm.

This cacophony burst into the coffee room as though shot from a cannon. Without ado, Kenton stood up, swinging Maris to the floor. She stood, trying to bundle her fair hair into some sort of order, while he attempted to achieve silence.

A short, plump, and very blond girl pushed the crying child, an infant of about two years of age, into Kenton's arms. The little body piked straight out, as though tacking a sailboat.

"My wife," Rigby said. "Lady Barrington."

"And I told her and told her that a little warm goose grease rubbed in careful like would relieve it, but she didn't pay me no mind," said a young woman who bore a remarkable resemblance, minus a few years and a few pounds, to the landlady. "It's not my fault that baby is possessed of a devil, is it?"

At this, the Spanish girl's shaky English broke down and she began throwing the sort of phrases that made Kenton glad Maris didn't understand Spanish.

"Pray be quiet, both of you," he said. *"Silencio! Silencio, por Dio."*

Maris, laughing at him, took the baby from his arms and began to joggle it gently. "There, there, little man. What's the matter, then?"

"He cry and cry," his mother said, changing with bewildering rapidity from shrieking virago to concerned parent. "I t'ink milk in this place not like him. It smell of onions."

Maris had noticed that the baby's stomach seemed rather distended. "We'll find something in the kitchen to ease him," she promised.

"I told 'er goose grease," the landlady's daughter put in. Maris had noticed from the smell that this remedy had already been tried.

"Enough about the goose grease," Maris said, giving the baby back to his mother. "We shall manage without it. Come with me, Lady Barrington."

"You will call me Yolanda," the Spanish bride said with the same air of decision that marked her mother-in-law. "We are to be friends."

Maris stopped on the doorstep. "The chaise won't hold us all, Kenton. Will you make the arrangements for everyone?"

He bowed. Turning to the landlady's daughter, he ordered two pints of ale to toast his lady in. Sir Rigby would never be his dearest friend, but he had been the indirect cause of all his happiness. He'd share a drink with him. Besides, the man looked as if he needed it. "A fine son," he said.

"It's a daughter. I didn't know Yolanda was pregnant when I left Spain."

"Your mother will be delighted."

Rigby brightened. "That's true. So am I, actually. You should get married, Danesby. There's nothing like it."

Yolanda Barrington had been very grateful for Maris's assistance with her child but had scorned the idea that she needed anyone to soften the news of her existence. Maris, knowing Lady Barrington's yearning for a grandchild, knew Yolanda already had the only advocate she would need and so let Rigby and his bride go on their way without a qualm.

In the dark, riding home cuddled up close to Kenton in the inn's hired gig, Maris felt a great sense of peace, as though she'd come to a resting place. It was not the end of a journey, but a pause before she began on a new path. With Kenton to aid her, she wondered how high she could climb.

They stopped in the square and it was some time before Maris even thought of going into her house. "It's really your house, isn't it?" she asked.

"Yes. I leased it to Dominic."

"But Tremlow said . . . Tremlow? Your butler?"

"My butler. And Dominic is now the Duke of Saltaire. It's a long story, full of second cousins once removed, attainders, and attorneys. You'll hear all about it later."

"Later is better," she said, drawing his head down to hers once more.

Though there wasn't much room in the gig, after a little, Kenton put Maris into the farthest corner and sat with as much distance between them as was possible. "I shall go to London tomorrow for a special license. How soon can you and Miss Menthrip return to Finchley?"

"For this, she would travel all night."

"And you?"

She laughed, softly and tenderly, stealing her hand into his. "I wanted to go to Gretna, remember?"

Kenton reached for her again but restrained himself to Maris's expressed disappointment. "I've bent my gentlemanly code far enough for one night," he said, tucking his hands firmly under his thighs to keep them from wandering. Unfortunately, that left him with no means of defense.

This time, she called a halt. "Is that a constable?" she asked, peering into the darkness under the oak.

"I'm surprised it isn't an outraged moralist," Kenton said, touching his cravat. So much for his reputation as a well-dressed man. "You had better go in. What excuse did you give to Miss Menthrip for your leaving with Barrington?"

"A whist party that needed an extra player. Which explains why I seemed to be eloping in pale coffee silk."

"Which becomes you very well," he said.

"Well, it's sadly crushed now, isn't it? I shall have to hold my cloak together and hurry upstairs."

"In for a penny, in for a pound," Kenton said, slipping an arm around her. The pale coffee silk warmed like flesh under his hands. He felt giddy, like a boy in the throes of his first affair, and yet sanctified, knowing that this was his true wife in every way but the lawful one. That would happen as soon as humanly and legally possible.

"I'll come to visit you in the morning. Can you leave for Finchley by noon? That way, I can escort you until your halt for the night. Then I'll head toward London and you'll have only a half day's journey on. We can hire outriders at the George in Shifton."

"I think so," she said hesitantly.

"What is it?" Kenton asked, alive to every shade of nuance in her voice.

"Couldn't we be married in London? I'll write Mother . . ."

"We could. But, well, all my family has married at Finchley, ever since the beginning. Except my great-grandfather but we don't discuss him."

"If it's a tradition that we flout at our peril, then of course we shall marry in Finchley."

"Why not?"

"It's only that . . . I've heard them talking at home about you and what it is to be lord and lady of the manor."

"You will make a splendid lady of the manor."

"But they expect you to bring home some amazingly accomplished creature to be your lady. Someone to guide them and be an example and a Lady Bountiful. And what are you bringing them? Me—the girl next door whom they've known all their lives and, to be truthful, don't rate very highly. What will they think?"

Kenton laughed. "They'll think it is the greatest romance of the century."

And so they did.

ABOUT THE AUTHOR

Cynthia Pratt lives in Maryland. She is currently working on her next Zebra Regency romance, which will be published in August 2004.

More Regency Romance
From Zebra